Stuck Under the Mistletoe

THE NAUGHTY LIST

GEORGIA COFFMAN

Stuck Under the Mistletoe © 2022 GEORGIA COFFMAN

All rights reserved.

This is a work of fiction. Names, places, characters, and events are fictitious in every regard. Any similarities to actual events and persons, living or dead, are purely coincidental. Any trademarks, service marks, product names, or named features are assumed to be the property of their respective owners, and are used only for reference. There is no implied endorsement if any of these terms are used. Except for review purposes, the reproduction of this book in whole or part, electronically or mechanically, constitutes a copyright violation.

Prologue © 2022 by Mae Harden and Chelle Sloan, used with permission

Editing by Amanda Cuff, Word of Advice Editing
Cover Design by Mae Harden

For all the sweet Christmas movie fans who always wish for a little more spice ;)

Prologue

ONE WOULD HAVE to be living under a rock to not have seen the now-viral interview featuring beloved Adored Network actress Hollie Berry and Lyle Tucker on *Wake Up LA*.

The country is divided on Berry's reactions to Tucker's questions and her abrupt firing from Adored Network. The girl next door known for her sweet and romantic Christmas movies shocked millions when she loudly proclaimed that she was "claiming her coal" instead of apologizing for her off-brand behavior at a Vegas nightclub.

What does that phrase mean? Why has it become the top trending hashtag on every social media platform? Why has #ClaimYourCoal become the new battle cry of women around the world?

US Daily has received the full video of the interview between Berry and Tucker and has transcribed it below. This includes the un-aired portion where Berry stormed off the set.

Is Berry justified in her actions? Are Adored Network and Tucker? You can decide for yourself.

LYLE TUCKER: Thank you for being on the show. I must say, not everyone can be as beautiful as you, especially after the weekend you had.

HOLLIE BERRY: Thanks for having me! It's great to be here.

LT: The last forty-eight hours for you I'm sure have been a whirlwind. Do you have anything to say regarding your behavior this weekend? Some are saying that your actions may have put you on Santa's naughty list...

HB: (Laughing) The naughty list... It was my best friend's bachelorette party, but the images and videos were taken completely out of context.

LT: Then please, what was the original context? Because from what the world has seen in a video that now has more than three million views, it looks like you were having sex on stage with a male stripper.

HB: Well, that's a little dramatic considering I was fully clothed and he was still in his Tarzan loincloth. There was absolutely no sex involved with our weekend.

LT: Thank you for bringing that up. The selfie of you next to a half-naked man is a little off-brand for you, don't you think? You're the sweetheart of the Adored Network, known for their sweet and romantic movies. What has Adored said to you about your behavior in terms of the video and photo?

HB: The dancer is a fan of my movies. He and his husband watch them every year on the network. He asked for a selfie afterward. I have *never* told a fan no if they want a picture. And as far as the network goes, Adored hasn't said a thing. My private life is mine to do what I want with, as long as it doesn't go against my contract. And attending a dance performance certainly isn't forbidden.

LT: A dance performance? You call men dancing for women in nothing but their underwear a dance performance? Sounds more like a strip club to me.

HB: It wasn't a strip club. Naked Heat is a dance performance. It's not like we were there to throw dollar bills around.

LT: Even so, you had to know that the Adored Network

would not be happy with how you are spending your free time.

HB: Well, I think that's kind of the point. It's MY free time. And I wanted to spend MY free time celebrating my best friend's bachelorette party.

LT: Actually, we have a bit of breaking news here. I've just been handed a press release from the Adored Network saying that they are terminating your contract with the network for breaking a morality clause and are canceling your next three movies. What is your reaction to this?

HB: ... Um, obviously I don't know anything about that.

LT: Well, it's true. Viewers at home, you are now seeing a photo of the press release that was just sent out by Adored.

HB: (long pause) I'm sorry, this is the press release? Like they just sent this out without even notifying me first? If that's true, then I guess you'll need to speak to my lawyer. I don't think I should comment on this without—

LT: But Hollie, you have to have some feelings about this? These movies you make for Adored made your career and, frankly, are the only reason people even know who you are. You have to have something to say about this decision?

HB: Yeah, I have some feelings. Pretty specific feelings. If that's an actual press release, I think it's pretty (expletive removed) up that they would do that without contacting me first.

LT: Please, Hollie, watch your tone and words. And of course it's an actual press release. Do you think we would lie to you? We aren't the ones being questioned about our moral standards.

HB: MY moral standards? I've lived in Hollywood for 20 years with a squeaky-clean image. Do you have any idea how hard that is? I don't party; I don't sleep around. I do my job, and I'm good at it. God forbid I go to a bachelorette party! How about your moral standards? You like publicly shaming women for something every man in America has done. How does that line up with your moral compass?

LT: My moral compass isn't being questioned here. I wasn't the one who, as it has been described by numerous media outlets and tabloids, dry humped a man in front of hundreds of other women. What kind of message does that say to other women or young girls who consider you a role model? Is that the kind of moral standard you want to set for them?

HB: Yeah, you know what? It is! If women want to take control of their sexuality, I say go for it! Why do men like you get to decide what's okay? I didn't dry hump anyone in Vegas, but if I had, that would be my choice. You want to know about *my* message to women and girls? Here it is. Go out there and make the world your (expletive deleted). If this puts me on the naughty list then so be it. I'll take all the coal. Hell, I'll proudly claim my coal!

LT: You just lost your biggest contract. You are a viral video. Do you really think encouraging women and girls to, as you said, claim their coal, is the best thing you can do right now?

HB: No. The best thing I can do is this... (muffled noises) I'll show you what claiming my coal looks like, you ignorant... (muffled noises)

At this point in the interview, Hollie Berry removed her microphone. So while we can't know exactly what she said to Mr. Tucker as a parting shot, the middle finger salute she gave him as she stormed off stage was pretty clear.

CHAPTER
One

KATIE

I ALWAYS THOUGHT if I were involved in a scandal it would be because Robert Downey Jr. and I were caught doing it on the beach in Malibu.

In my fantasy, he wasn't married, so it wasn't adultery. Rather, it was just some good old-fashioned public indecency with the sexy actor.

My more plausible thought was that I'd grow up and out of the children's TV show I starred in. Then, once I was old enough, I'd be caught doing drugs or making out with one of the producers.

Thankfully, I got out of the public eye before I hit my teens. While I escaped ridicule and criticism then—very few national magazines cared about a lanky ten-year-old leaving the TV industry—I'm not so lucky now.

I only wish my cringey reality was more glamorously scandalous.

I turn the TV off and silence the rampant lies the local news anchors were ignorantly slinging at me. But ignorant or not, they have the upper hand right now.

This is bad.

At first, it was just a few pictures littered across the World Wide Web. I had to actively search to find them. But when more details of the situation were unearthed by a couple semiviral videos—thanks a lot, social media—local media outlets grabbed hold of my story in their sleazy hands and ran like the wind.

If I had done anything truly awful, I'd say I deserve what's coming to me, but I didn't. I was simply doing my damn job.

In the bathroom, I set my phone next to the sink and put it on speaker while I finish getting ready.

"I haven't gotten to your case yet, ma'am." My lawyer's voice crackles through like he's using a landline.

Do they still make those? If they do, he definitely has one. I didn't see it the last time I was in his office, but I was too frazzled to even notice the piece of lettuce stuck between my teeth, let alone a contraption from the past.

After all, I was too worried and anxious over the fact that a student's father had filed a lawsuit against me.

Leaning toward the mirror, I blend in what Kylie Cosmetics calls the "Head Over Heels" matte lipstick and hope it brings me luck tonight.

"I called you a week ago, and you said you'd look it over that same day," I press and quietly smack my lips together as my stomach churns.

"I didn't, though." Loud chewing echoes from his end like he's in the middle of dinner. It's still early for a Friday night, but maybe he's just having a snack.

In the middle of our freaking phone call.

This is the *fantastic* service I'm able to afford with my teacher's salary.

"What's the big deal? So you showed some pornographic art in your class." He wheezes, the sound similar to someone choking, but to my misfortune, he's fine. "All art is pornographic."

"I'm being sued!" I screech. As I stare at the phone, wishing I had the superpower to set it on fire, I slump against the edge of the counter with the weight of my situation heavy on my heart. "It's not the school being sued. *I'm* being sued by a disgruntled parent like this is personal. And the news is making up such terrible lies about me. They're making me out to be a monster."

"Well, were you sleeping with this guy, or something?"

"No!" Hands shaking, I drop the lipstick into the sink, and it leaves pink streaks along the white ceramic. Why is everything such a fucking mess?

"You said it might be personal, so I had to check."

"What about my check? I already paid you for your legal services, and you're not doing what we agreed on."

"I'm doing everything I can, Miss." A ding interrupts this super helpful conversation. "That's my hot pock—I mean, my next client. I'll be in touch, especially with the bill for this consultation."

"I'm not paying you for this call. You didn't—"

I glance at the phone screen and realize he's already off the call.

"Fuck," I mutter and grab a bath towel from the floor to wipe the sink with. Then I march back into my bedroom, where I fling myself onto the bed and stare at the ceiling, phone still in my outstretched palm hanging off the edge.

With another exasperated exhale, I dial my mother.

"Hi, darling." Her voice sings throughout my solitary bedroom. She sounds perfectly at ease. With the time difference between me in New York and her in LA, she's probably just getting out of her standing facial appointment, so it makes sense that she sounds this happy. "Say hi to your sister."

I grimace as she makes obnoxious kissing sounds, which I

assume are for her well-groomed Pomeranian named Cinny —aka, *not* my sister.

"I've been thinking about you, Katie," my mom continues, and if she hadn't specifically said my name, I would've believed she was still talking to the dog.

My eyebrows shoot up. That's a first, and I wasn't even recording it for when I need proof that she does, in fact, care about me on a deep level. I would need it to keep me warm when she inevitably forgets to send me a Christmas card.

"How are you? You mentioned a difficult parent the last time we spoke," she says.

I huff a humorless laugh as I pull myself to sit upright. "He's not just difficult, Mom. He's suing me."

She gasps like it's the first she's hearing of this. In reality, I told her last Friday during our weekly chat. What she didn't know then was that the local news stations have picked up the story, so I fill her in on this sordid tidbit as well. After I'm finished, I get more gasps from her.

"This simply will not do, darling. Contrary to what others in Hollywood say, bad press is definitely not always a good thing. What is your lawyer doing about this?"

"Umm…" I bite my quivering lip, then remember my lipstick and immediately release it. I'm sure Kylie does not recommend a big tooth-wide streak in one of her cosmetic masterpieces.

"You have a good lawyer, right? I'm telling you—a good lawyer makes all the difference. It's how I ended up with so much alimony after your father decided he wanted to live in South Africa and forgot to invite us. You were too young to remember, but my lawyer is the one who got us through it. So, rest assured. Your lawyer will get you out of this pickle in no time."

"For sure. My lawyer is… totally great. Doesn't smell like bleu cheese… at all," I stammer.

"Cheese? Oh, God. Don't remind me. I started a strict nondairy diet in preparation for a callback I received. It's for a powdered milk commercial, and let's face it—no woman has my curves if she's living off fake milk, so I have to look the part. What am I saying? You remember what show business is like, darling. It's ruthless out here."

And we're done with my "pickle." We might've set a record as to how long we talked about me before she mentioned her auditions or my dad running off to another country without us.

After I got out of the spotlight, she stepped into it, transitioning from producer to actress practically overnight. She's been determined to make at least one of us Bumble women famous ever since. It's her way of "sticking it" to my father, as she often says.

"Listen, Mom, I need to go."

"Of course, of course."

"I have a date," I blurt and hold my breath for a positive reaction.

But unsurprisingly, she merely gives me the same warning she always does. "A date? What a marvelous way to have fun on a Friday night. Just remember to be yourself, and enjoy yourself too. No need for anything serious at your age, or ever, as you can see how well that worked out for me."

I offer a stiff laugh—my usual response—and promise to call her soon. In our case, that means next Friday. It's our unofficial ritual.

Before I hang up, I also wish her good luck on her audition, but she doesn't return the sentiment regarding the very serious allegations against me.

I check my watch and find I have a few minutes before I need to leave, so I slink onto the end of my unmade bed and stare at my closet. The only thing I see is the shimmery gold dress hanging front and center. When I found it in a store in Manhattan, I had to get it for my friend Tracy's Christmas party.

I bought it in preparation for the holiday season when I was excited for it. But instead of bringing me cheer, this December has dumped nothing but one shitshow after another on me.

Spots blink across my vision, blurring the outline of the dress.

I'm angry.

Hurt.

Humiliated.

All because I was trying to help and encourage my students to be bold, creative, and true to themselves.

I've been a high school art teacher for over three years, and I've hosted just as many art shows. Every November, I help the students come up with "their masterpiece," and then we showcase them for family and friends. It's a night to bring the community together over something they all love—their kids.

Parents sign up to bring snacks, and I bake apple cookies. It's the one time a year I actually use the cookie tray in my kitchen.

It's fun—normally.

This time, one girl painted parts of the female body, and I displayed it, proud of my student for exploring her creativity. Not everyone agreed with me, though.

Horace Williams guffawed the second he saw it, covered his teenage son's eyes, and stormed out of the gym, threatening to sue me on his way out.

Unfortunately for me, he's a man of his word.

Standing on my heels, I straighten my back, pulling my posture into its upright position as if I'm a seat on a plane, and I take off across the living room, the smell of cinnamon floating from a wallflower plug-in. The festive scent complements the twinkling Christmas lights strewn along the edge of my counter, and the gingerbread men in chef's hats decorating each corner of the kitchen follow my every stride.

It's the only joyful spot in my apartment since this lawsuit halted all my holiday plans. I don't even have my tree up yet, and I'm about two weeks late on it. I'm the type to put it up when the clock strikes midnight on Thanksgiving, and not a second later.

But not this year.

Blowing out a frustrated exhale, cinnamon-dioxide leaving my parted pink lips, I'm ready for a night out.

This date is coming at the perfect time—I need the distraction.

As I pull up to the front of the swanky restaurant in Manhattan, I check the address on my phone to confirm this is the right place, and I exit the Uber. In the same text with the address, Griffin apologizes for not picking me up himself, but he got hung up at work and will meet me here.

I've never even seen a picture of him, but the guy's already earned brownie points for saying sorry. I'm not high-maintenance or extremely traditional, but a considerate gentleman never goes out of style in my book.

I smooth my black dress over the cinched waist that flatters my figure—I bought it specifically for tonight.

Tracy said this blind date would get me out of my funk, and I believe my best friend since college is onto something. Of course, she's biased and overly optimistic since Griffin is her brother, but I trust her.

I just hope I'm not underdressed. This place is a lot fancier than any restaurant I've ever even heard of, let alone personally experienced. I almost find comfort in the decorations, but even those are classy as hell. Everything is gold—trees, centerpieces, and servers' ties. It looks nothing like my plush gingerbread men scattered haphazardly around my apartment like a third grader got bored in there.

Teetering on my heels in front of the door, I buy myself time, hesitant to go in and find out I am, indeed, far too inferior for this place.

And then there's Griffin, lawyer extraordinaire and the most eligible bachelor Tracy knows. Which isn't saying much, since my friend just moved to New York City a few months ago. She hasn't had time to meet anyone for herself, let alone for me.

I can do this.

I *need* to do this.

The last date I went on was with Tommy, the PE teacher at my school. Although he was nice—and seriously hotter than the sun—he dumped me because he wasn't at peace with his divorce. While I appreciated his honesty, I could've done without the lame pat on my arm like I was one of his students who got picked last for a game of kickball.

So, yeah, I freaking need this.

With one last deep breath, I enter the restaurant, and I'm immediately greeted by a woman with red lips and a sleek ponytail. I offer her a weak smile before she spins on her glossy black pumps and leads me to a table.

Griffin is just a guy.

Even if there are seven forks next to my plate, they're still just forks. If Ariel from *The Little Mermaid* can survive a fancy meal, so can I.

Except twenty minutes pass, and there's no sign of my blind date. He hasn't responded to my message telling him I've arrived. No other missed call or text.

I don't have anything from Tracy, either, unless I count the obscene number of winky face emojis I received earlier. She was excited, so she obviously didn't know her brother wouldn't be coming tonight.

Did his work tie him up longer than he'd expected? Maybe he lost track of time.

I twirl my phone around in circles on the table and jump when it clashes against one of four forks—better than seven, I guess.

The server clears his throat, spearing his gaze from the

phone to my reddening cheeks. "It's been almost thirty minutes," he says, and although there's a hint of a question in his snide tone, it's still only a statement.

"Has it?" I feign a mixture of surprise and confusion, but I know good and well it's been exactly thirty-two minutes with no sign of Griffin.

"Would you like an appetizer with your wine?" He gives me a tight, exasperated smile, which appears more painful than it did when I asked for the cheapest glass of white wine after the first fifteen minutes alone.

I give the menu a quick scan, barely recognizing five words in the complex lexicon of fine dining. Even if I knew what and how to order, I can't be the girl who eats alone at a place like this.

I wouldn't be drinking alone, either, but I had to order something while I waited. People were starting to stare, although that could've just been my paranoia.

In any case, wine is never a bad idea.

As I fold the menu closed, I suppress a growl of protest from my stomach and shake my head in response to the uptight server.

"Very well." He whirls around on his heel and marches away, taking his attitude and my dignity with him.

I've been stood up.

I can make excuses for Griffin and his work all night, but I'm not stupid. I know the truth.

On top of my public humiliation, a guy who's never even met me has already decided he doesn't want anything to do with me.

Fantastic.

After another fifteen minutes of the crushing weight of my reality, I down the rest of my white wine, toss a twenty and a five onto the table, and slide off my chair. As I maneuver through the crowd, I try not to drool over decadent plates of assorted seafood, salads, and other items I'd need a professional cooking course to label.

It all looks so delicious, and I can't believe I'm about to grab a two-dollar slice of cheese pizza along my walk of shame—except I won't even be getting dirty sex out of this.

Just a sad stroll back to my lonely apartment.

When I arrive home, I trudge toward my bed, kicking my shoes off in two directions along the way, and I grab my laptop before snuggling underneath the covers to warm myself up.

US Daily is on my front search engine page, with a picture of Hollie Berry underneath a rather shaming headline. To match, the image they use is less than flattering. She's usually shown with long blonde hair flowing over her shoulders in glamorous waves—the kind I can never attain, no matter what products I use—but this image shows her hair in a tangled mess on top of her head. Her lipstick is smeared in one corner too, and it looks nothing like her.

Is it her?

I click on the link, and it leads me to an interview with Lyle Tucker, which involves some questions regarding a Vegas scandal. The Adored Network star and I have a lot in common.

Minus the hair, of course.

I can relate to Hollie on a level that reaches my soul.

As I read through the transcript, I know I came to the right place for a little motivation, even if by accident. I could call my friend Erin—the most positive person I know—but Hollie Berry's no-nonsense monologue does the trick to flip my sour mood on its ass.

Despite the lawsuit and my blind date no-show, there's nothing wrong with *me*. I'm smart. Creative. Fun.

I have a respectable job. Despite what they're saying about me, I'm great at it too. I also possess many talents, including the ability to gobble two slices of pizza while maneuvering a

Friday night in Manhattan like a freaking champ. I didn't get a single drop of grease on my little black dress or anything.

But more than any of that, I'm a strong woman, and I'm not going to let asshole men bring me down—not my lawyer, my no-show, or the angry Horace Williams.

This is my life, and I'm going to live it however I see fit.

This Christmas, I'm going to claim *my* fucking coal.

CHAPTER
Two

GRIFFIN

"YOU STOOD HER UP?" my sister screeches.

I pull the phone away while she scolds me with the longest string of curse words known to man. Toward the end of her long-winded rant, she oddly attacks my inability to throw a baseball very fast.

"You know I have a bad shoulder."

She talks over me until the pitch of her tone reaches inhumane decibels.

Fuck.

This is worse than the time I interrupted her "date" with Brian Spaulding in high school. No teenage sister of mine was going to date the school's douchebag—not on my watch. I was doing her a favor, but she didn't see it that way.

Thankfully, Brian incriminated himself by hooking up with someone else about an hour after I kicked him out of our house.

If Tracy would've trusted me to start with, I could've saved her the heartbreak.

But even all these years later, she still thinks she knows better than me.

I finally get a word in when she pauses to catch her breath. "You set me up with the city's pariah, Trace. Her story is on half a dozen local news stations, which I thought was nearly impossible to accomplish in this city. It's not like Kansas, where anything out of the ordinary, including the Piggly Wiggly stocking a new brand of flour, garners the media's attention."

This earns me a soft laugh. It's weak, but I heard it.

I hang my head, and a wavy tuft of tawny hair falls into my eyes. I usually keep my hair longer than some of the guys I work with, but I might be overdue for a trim.

I did shave this morning, so that has to count for something. Tracy's always telling me to take care of myself. If she were standing in front of me, I suspect she'd give me a pat on the back for my appearance, at the very least.

Pinching the bridge of my nose, I ask, "Were you trying to get back at me for setting you up with Sneezy Steve? Because I already told you, I didn't know he had such bad allergies."

"He sneezed in my mashed potatoes, Griffin. My *mashed potatoes*," she repeats in a whisper layered with disbelief that such cruelty exists.

She has no idea.

With what I do for a living, I've seen it all, and most days, I wish the worst thing these dirtbags did was fling their germs in my carbs.

"Katie was perfect for you," my naively optimistic sister insists.

"She encouraged her teenage students to create pornographic paintings, and I'm a family lawyer. How is that perfect for me?" I chide as I arrange papers into a neat stack on my desk.

I was able to finish drafting a will since I didn't go to

dinner with Katie last night. The free time gave me the opportunity to forge ahead.

Victory.

"You know that's not what happened, and you of all people should *know* there's always another side to the story."

I work my jaw back and forth. This gives me pause, but it's not enough for me to relent.

"I need to finish getting things ready for tonight." She sighs, but it's not a normal, casual sound. The drawn-out exhale is filled with disappointment. She might as well have said she thought I was better than this, and guilt gnaws at my stomach like a bad virus.

"Speaking of…" I hang my head.

"Don't tell me you're not coming to my party."

Great. This call has been full of one delightful topic after another. It's just what I needed after a work week from Hell and finding out the blind date I was extremely excited about was one that could sully my reputation and cost me business.

I went so far as to make reservations at my favorite swanky establishment, a restaurant I only experience during special occasions, but it was wasted.

"I'm swamped with work. I'm making progress, but Warren gave me two more cases to start on. I still have a full night ahead of me before I can enjoy what's left of the weekend." I squeeze my eyes closed and use the heel of my palms to dig into each, but it does nothing to curb the sting biting at each one. I've been staring at my computer for too long.

"That asshole never does any of his own work, does he?" Tracy curses my boss under her breath, then sighs again. This one is a little less disappointed than before, so I call it a win.

After I apologize, I promise to see her tomorrow for brunch, but she makes no such guarantee.

"It depends on how mad I still am at you for standing Katie up first, now me."

"I know just the right red velvet waffles to make sure you

forgive me," I say, ruthlessly bribing my own sister to like me again.

"Deal," she grinds out before we end the call.

She and I don't argue or disagree enough to reach this degree of groveling, so the rules are unclear here. Thankfully, I'm quick on my feet and know how to diffuse the tension. Red velvet waffles could fix any problem where Tracy is involved.

Bonus—they're the perfect cheat meal for me. Miles, my friend and personal trainer, agrees.

In any case, I've had plenty of practice with conflict resolution, considering how many volatile couples I've worked with. In fact, I assume the role of therapist more often than I care to lately.

Perhaps the sad reality of so many marriages and their demise is why I've never walked down the aisle myself.

Sure, sometimes a couple I work with is amicable and show each other the respect we all deserve, but when this is not the case, so much hatred consumes them that they can't tell their right foot from their left. The animosity toward each other frequently gets in the way of my job, but nothing deters me.

I'm a professional, and it's why I didn't go on the date last night.

My sister might think I'm an asshole because of it, and she's not completely wrong, but as long as I still sleep soundly at night, I'm fine.

Which I do, and I am.

I can't let anything or anyone soil the reputation I've worked for years to build. With so many other family law offices here in the city, the competition is fierce. Any tiny mishap could hurt the firm, and I have more than just myself to worry about.

At the top of that list are the partners. They would kill me if I stepped out of line. They already make it their mission to, unofficially, keep me beneath them. As an outsider—aka, non-New Yorker—they're far too quick to point out how inferior and less competent I am because of it. It's why they give me the simpler cases. Why I bury my head in divorces involving few assets and rarely any children to be tangled up in custody agreements.

In sum, they give me the cases they deem unworthy of their superior expertise.

I've had to work extra hard to even walk through the door of this suite. If any of my colleagues learn I almost went on a date with Katie Bumble, the current walking, talking, trending scandal, I'd be skating on thin ice around here.

I can't let a stupid romantic endeavor hold me back from climbing from associate to partner.

Tracy doesn't understand the pressure I'm under, but she was right about one thing—there are always more sides to every story, including the one where I stood up my sister's best friend. None of it is Tracy's concern, though.

"Chase!" Warren, one of the partners, bursts into my office with green garland draped over his disheveled suit. "We're going out, and Mia wanted me to ask if you're going to join us for once? There's no better time to start living than Christmastime!"

A commotion follows from behind him, and through a gap between his shoulder and the doorframe, I catch flashes of familiar faces, including our receptionist and a couple paralegals.

I'm surprised this many people are here on a Saturday night. To be honest, I didn't even notice more than two others in the hall earlier.

I glance at the time and realize I haven't gotten up in almost two hours—a new record. "Shit," I mutter, standing behind my desk and stretching my tight back. "Not tonight, Warren."

"See? I told you he's too busy," the tall Christmas tree of a man says to the group and bursts into laughter. Next to him, Mia slouches, then flinches when Warren snaps his fingers. "Oh, wait! He's afraid of the cinnamon dust in the air."

"Glad you find my cinnamon allergy so amusing," I say.

"Don't be such a sourpuss." My completely *professional* boss slurs his words and waves me off. "Get back to what you're good at—the work. Leave the fun up to us."

"Gladly," I mutter as the similarly decorated crew follows Warren toward the elevators like a holiday conga line, cheering on their way out.

He obviously went a little crazy with the pre-party drinking. I'd hate to witness end-of-the-night Warren, but I won't be doing any such thing. While I do have an allergy to this season's *most wonderful* spice, it's not the reason I won't be joining my co-workers.

There are more important things on my to-do list to accomplish before my head hits the pillow tonight.

I don't hear the elevator beep with its arrival, but I know when it closes, since silence claims the office.

I don't have to check to know I'm alone. That I'm the only person who's partying with his work rather than at the nearest bar.

The funny thing about it is that I'd like to go out, have a drink, and maybe meet a nice woman, but my job is important to me. If I still need to pay my dues after all I've accomplished, so be it.

I'll do whatever it takes.

But an hour later, the silence finally wins. I can't focus. Not with my nagging thoughts of everyone having fun but me.

I tap the side of my stack, straightening the edges of the documents into a neat tower, then grab my jacket and join the rest of the world.

CHAPTER

GRIFFIN

AS I CROSS THE STREET, Tracy's decorated brownstone comes into view. A few people hang outside of it with cigarettes in their hands, twinkling lights hung above them around the doorframe, the two windows on either side of it, and the railing along the steps.

As I near her festive stoop, I hear the faint notes of Christmas music and cheers from all the guests.

From the looks and sounds of it, her holiday party is in full swing, and I've made it just in time to enjoy the liveliest part. It makes me glad I came out tonight, not that Warren could see me now.

His unwarranted dismissal of me earlier pissed me off, but who needs him and the rest? There's a party right here.

As soon as my sister opens the door, her expression falls from elated to surprised and settles on a distorted mix of confusion and panic.

"I thought you said you weren't coming," she says, but it comes out as more of a question.

"Hello to you too," I tease and lean in to kiss her cheek,

glimpsing a group of people flitting across the hall behind her. "Is this how you've greeted all your guests tonight? If so, I'm surprised so many of them stayed."

"Right. Right." She nods and shuffles to the side to make room for me.

As I cross the snowman welcome mat into the warmth of her house, I survey the crowd, most of whom are dressed to the nines in sequined dresses and crisp suits. Most of them also wear Santa hats, light-up headbands, and the like. My sister herself wears a belt across the waistband of her leather skirt, which reads "Sleigh."

A swarm of guests huddled around the makeshift bar catches my attention. Hung in front of the table is a sign that reads "Drink Up Grinches," and next to it, a couple takes pictures by the lit-up Christmas tree.

I inhale deeply and confirm there's no cinnamon in the air. This time of year is difficult for me, given how popular the spice is. Everyone around the world seems to think cinnamon is such a staple of the season. They act like if they don't burn every such candle on sale at Bath and Body Works, or bake every kind of cinnamon muffin, we just can't live on.

If I could find the asshole responsible for promoting it as a fall and winter necessity, I'd give them a hostile piece of my mind.

Tracy always remembers, though. We haven't lived in the same city—we've barely seen each other at all—in years, but she remembers.

I turn to her as she shuts the door with her heel like she's kicking the cold out on its ass, and instantly, the chill disappears.

"How do you know all these people?" I ask. "You just moved to New York, and already, you have more friends than I do."

She rubs her hands down both arms, warming herself up as she glares at me. "I'm a lot nicer to people than you are."

I scoff. "Don't start with me about the blind date again."

"I talked to Katie earlier and told her you wouldn't be here tonight, so just stay out of her way, okay?"

"She's here?" My stomach lurches.

Fuck.

I didn't even think about her being here, but I should've known. After all, she and Tracy are close friends. Up until five minutes ago, I actually thought Katie was the only friend my sister had in the city.

Looking around now, it's clear Trace is doing just fine.

She peers over my shoulder. "I need to play the good hostess and put more cookies out. Mingle. Have a drink. I'll come find you in a bit." She brushes past me but stops to hold her finger in my face, eyes very similar to mine boring into my soul. "And be nice to Katie."

"I don't even know what she looks like. How am I supposed to prepare myself?"

"Here's an idea—just be nice to everyone."

I mumble a curse, but it's mostly to her back since she's already scurried off like her guests are threatening to leave if she doesn't put more cookies out.

If I listen carefully, I can hear the faint tunes of holiday music, but it's muffled by the buzzing chatter of people letting loose tonight.

Which is what I need to do, starting with a drink.

As I pour myself a Scotch neat, I glance around the room, suddenly wishing I'd gone straight home after work. I came out to have fun and play nice with my sister, but it's going to blow up in my face if I run into Katie.

I wish I had a better idea of what she looked like. Tracy insisted on upholding the *magical* mystery of a blind date, saying it would be more exciting that way.

She didn't show Katie a picture of me, either, not that she had very many options to choose from. I hate having my picture taken. The last one was a professional headshot for the firm's website, and the one before that was probably from a college friend's wedding five years ago.

My meddling sister—and hopeless romantic with an aptitude for dramatic flare—told me to avoid the news too. I did, for the most part, and in doing so, I never caught an image of Katie.

But I couldn't ignore what was said altogether.

I sneak glimpses over my shoulder in search of the disgraced art teacher, but it's useless. With nothing to go on, picking out Katie is a lot more difficult than detective shows make it seem. I don't have an expert IT team waiting for my signal to run facial recognition, nor do I have years of training to weed her out of the crowd.

So, I rely on stereotypes.

In my head, a high school art teacher is a bubbly free-spirit. It fits the bill since my sister thought such a personality type would be the best way to melt the glue holding my rigid exterior together.

I also imagine an art enthusiast to have frizzy hair, although I'm not sure why. It's just what comes to mind. A woman fitting this description comes into view, and right before I turn my back to avoid any damning eye contact, someone calls her by the name of Ruth.

With a sigh of relief, I continue my aimless search, imagining paint or ink blotches on her clothes as a dog owner might their pet's hair. It's why I don't have any animals at home, unless I count the ceramic cat my sister gave me for my birthday.

It was her special way of getting me to crack a smile, but all I want to do is crack the damn cat into pieces. It stares at me every morning with its creepy, hollow eyes. I've only refrained from doing it any harm because it was a gift from my sister.

I've just read the sign next to the row of drinks, which says "If the lights are lit, so are we!" when I hear someone to my side.

"Shoot," she huffs, and it's followed by a few thuds.

Leaning beside the table is a woman with tresses of blonde hair, a string of gaudy Christmas lights decorating the headband nestled in her thick and wavy locks. The gold dress she wears hugs her body with ease, and what draws me in next is the matching heel in her hand, which she smacks against the rug on the floor.

She groans and curses under her breath, seemingly unaware—or simply uncaring—that she's in a room full of people.

I respect that level of self-confidence.

After another sip of my stiff drink, I set down the glass, then crouch to meet her at eye level, succumbing to this intriguing distraction. "I'd ask what you're doing, but I think guessing would be more fun."

She blinks at me, and simultaneously, we straighten to our full height. Well, she's still only wearing one heel, so she's lopsided. Even so, she rises to meet my chin.

"What?" she asks, a deep flush of red coursing through her cheeks.

I point to the shoe in her hand, and understanding dawns, smoothing out the furrow in her brow.

Her smile spreads slowly. "Let's hear it, then. What's your first guess?"

"You're trying to get money out of it, but the bill is jammed in the painful-looking point." I study the death trap with a grimace. How does her foot actually fit in there? It's so cramped, I probably couldn't even fit two pencils inside, let alone five human toes.

She shakes her head.

"It's been extra naughty this year."

This earns me a burst of laughter, and I chuckle along with her.

"I'm trying to get a rock out of it, but your answer is

cuter."

"That's what I was going for—cute." I teeter on my heels, a coy grin tugging at my lips as I drink her in like I just drank my Scotch.

The dimples in her cheeks when she smiles are as charming as the smile itself, and when she peers up at me, her admiring gaze stuck on me, my mouth actually dries.

Her pale blue eyes are warm, but the black eyeliner sweeping across her top lid gives her an edge. It suggests she's not as innocent as one might think, and I find an embarrassing amount of pleasure in that notion.

"Right. Guys don't like to be called cute, do they? You're a stranger, though, so I can't tell you to your face that you're good-looking, or downright fucking hot. That would be inappropriate." She shrugs with obvious sarcasm, and a flirtatious twinkle blinks in her eyes.

Did she just call me fucking hot?

I might've been on the fence about coming here, but it was worth it if only for that compliment.

As she bends down again to collect her shoe, I beat her to it, falling to my knees with ease. With my ego this inflated, there's no stopping how smooth I am.

Scooping up the heel, I say, "Let me."

Her eyebrows shoot up. "Really?"

"It's the least I can do after such a compliment." I wink, and her cheeks turn as red as Santa Claus's suit.

I grip her hand and guide her to sit on the nearest armchair. The piece of furniture is adorned in blue and yellow flowers, and my sister herself admits she never uses it for anything other than decoration.

But it's serving a damn good purpose right now.

As I kneel before this interesting mystery woman, I try to focus on the odd shapes featured on the chair rather than how long it's been since I last touched a woman. Since I had my hands on a woman's soft skin or shared an evening with one in my bed.

I definitely focus on anything other than the exquisite way the sparkling gold dress clings to her body, or how the hem rides up both thighs as she leans back in the seat.

"You are such a gentleman," she says, a hint of surprise in her tone.

I cup her smooth calf and lift her leg high enough to slip her heel into place, careful not to flash the entire room, although I'd gladly accept a peek.

But doing so would be in direct contrast to what she just called me.

"That's a first," I say, and another chuckle springs free from my throat as I set her foot back down. "I'm usually called anything along the lines of an asshole and heartless jerk. My favorite was by a chef I once worked with, who said I was an amuse-*douche*."

She slides one delicate hand over her mouth as she giggles, and even with half her face covered, she's radiant.

With the corners of her eyes still crinkled, I take her other hand in mine, and we rise again in sync. It's already clear to me how compatible we are, even though we just met.

That's new.

"We need drinks." I turn around but keep her fingers entwined with mine for her to follow.

A red and green cloth is draped over the table, and several ornaments hang from the bottom. Many half-full bottles of booze are scattered on top, and I'm guessing they were arranged in neat rows before guests arrived. My sister and I have the organizational gene in common, but we definitely don't share the same taste in tacky Christmas signs.

"You have to try one of these cookies. I made them myself. I usually only bake them in November, but I thought—what the hell, I've already gone way out of my norm over the last month. Why stop now?" She holds up a plate, and although the excited expectation in her eyes is beyond adorable, I have to stop myself from devouring the entire batch.

"What kind are they?" I ask with caution.

"Apple cookies. I used…" She taps a manicured finger to her chin, the glittery red nail color popping against her porcelain complexion. It's almost enough to distract me from what she says next. "Brown sugar and cinnamon. They're my holiday specialty."

I smile around my frown, and I'm sure it's not a reflection of her previous compliment of me being *fucking hot*. "I'm sure they're fantastic, but unfortunately, I'm allergic to cinnamon." I take a step back for fear I'll get too close to my Kryptonite.

"Oh my God." She spins around so quickly, two cookies slide off the plate and onto the rug. Crumbs sprinkle onto a few people's shoes, but they don't seem to notice. I start to reach out to help her, but I again have to stop myself.

I can't touch them. It's bad enough that the spice is floating in the air around me, so I take several steps back until my shoulder comes into contact with the tree, causing the ornaments to jingle.

Once she's picked them up and dusted her hands off, she adjusts her holiday headband back into place on her head and joins me. "I'm so sorry. I didn't know."

She says something else, but it's muffled. She's cut off altogether by someone bumping into her, and a second person steps between us.

This corner of the room quickly crowds as two couples start dancing, so a small handful of us shuffle around the room to a comfortable—and cinnamon-free—spot. My new friend and I end up in the entryway to the living room.

"As I was trying to say, it must be hard to work in a restaurant with cinnamon around?" she says, raising her voice at the end in question.

"I don't work in a restaurant."

"You don't? You mentioned a chef before."

I tilt my head, then quickly remember I did say as much. "I'm a family lawyer. One of my clients last year was a chef."

"Oh." She shifts on her feet. I'd say she's more comfortable now that the rock is out of her heel, but in any case, those things are so tall and narrow, there's no way anyone would be at ease in them.

Then again, they make her legs look divine, so I can't complain.

In fact, the thought of seeing her in *only* those glittering shoes slams into me with the sudden force of a freight train. It's been too fucking long for me, and I'm wound tighter than the springs in the elf bobble heads smiling at us from the steps. There's one on each, staggered in the middle half of the stairs.

How much time did Tracy spend on these ridiculous decorations? I'd say she decorated only for this party, but my sister's always been overly enthusiastic when it comes to this time of year. I just haven't experienced it firsthand in recent years.

After clearing my throat, I ask, "What about you?"

At the same time, she asks, "So you must have an aversion to love too, then, huh?"

My lips twitch. This woman is very direct, and I have to admit, it's as refreshing as it is endearing.

"My question is more interesting, don't you think?" She flashes an impish grin.

"Agreed." I clink my glass against hers and take a sip. "I'm guessing you said that because you think I deal mostly with divorces. Many people assume as much, and it's true. I serve as the middleman to countless couples splitting up, but I handle happy families and their trusts as well."

She studies me, squinting her eyes in what seems to be contemplation like she suspects there's more to be said.

"But yes, I'm averse to love," I admit, my lips stained with

Scotch as the desolate confession eases through them. "I'm curious as to why you are as well."

She licks her lips, and I follow the movement, foregoing the subtlety of doing so too. I don't know her, but I can tell she doesn't seem to mind my perusal. Given the coy way she toys with her straw, I'd bet she wants me to notice.

She's flirting with me.

It hasn't been so long since I've gone out with a woman that I can't recognize the signs.

"It's not so much an aversion. For the time being, I've merely decided having fun is better than anything serious. Who cares about being on the nice list this year, anyway?" She presses her glass to her pink lips for a tantalizing sip.

"I couldn't agree more." I nod, using every ounce of self-control not to clap in celebration. This intoxicating woman is giving voice to my exact thoughts. "To having fun, then," I say as casually as possible.

But the stiffening appendage between my legs has a mind of its own.

She clinks her glass against mine in another toast, and as I tilt my drink back for a gulp, I notice the mistletoe hanging above us.

What a beautiful, beautiful plant.

Even more magnificent is its tradition.

"Speaking of fun…" I drop my attention back to her, and she meets my gaze. She obviously saw what I did and leans in until her tits graze my tie.

It's such a fucking tease.

The next few seconds feel like they happen in slow, excruciatingly arousing minutes.

Her hungry eyes drop to my mouth.

She angles her head to the side, inviting me in.

And I lose my grip on any restraint I possessed a moment ago, my body instantly hardening all over.

Cupping the back of her head, I guide her the rest of the way to capture her pretty mouth with mine.

Jesus Christ and Rudolph the Reindeer.

If holiday miracles had a taste, it would be wrapped into this kiss.

She's sweet and minty and spicy with a hint of citrus.

When she eases her body flush against mine, the sensual sigh escaping between her sweet lips makes my knees nearly buckle.

Mistletoe might be a fun tradition. A cute and innocent one for friends and maybe even strangers, as it is now. But there's nothing cute and innocent about this kiss.

I don't slow it down, either. Instead, I slip my greedy tongue between her perfect, sultry lips and devour more of her divine taste.

She grips my arm, meeting me swipe for swipe with her own roaming tongue, and when she tugs me closer, our glasses clink in an accidental toast.

The sound is soft, but it's enough to jolt us. As we jump back and lock eyes, I'm positive we're wearing matching satisfied smiles.

She chews on the inside of her cheek and nervously tucks a strand of hair behind her ear, and I'm left speechless.

Not a fucking word comes to mind.

I blink, and the rest of the room slowly reappears in my periphery, as do the thoughts in my head. "I should, um... I mean, if you're ever in the market for more fun... I should give you my number."

The rosy peaks of her cheeks grow rounder as they split into a bright smile, her dimples deep and giddy. It's the kind of grin that reaches deep into my chest and lets me know my life is about to change.

Swaying, she holds my gaze as she runs her hand up my forearm. "How should I save you in my contacts? Under amuse-*douche*, or...?"

I throw my head back and laugh—this woman is something else.

But the more I grin, the more difficult it physically becomes. Is my face... swelling?

It feels like the first time I had an allergic reaction to cinnamon, where my face grew to twice its normal size, and I broke into hives.

But I've been careful tonight.

I'm just swept away in my new mistletoe mistress—that's all.

"Griffin will do," I tell her, ready to follow it up with my number, but she snaps her attention away from her phone.

"Griffin?" She frowns, searching my face with utter—and mortified—confusion.

"Why do you say it like my name comes with a side of bullshit?" I joke, and my cheek suddenly itches. "What's your name?" I pull my phone out to keep my hands busy. Otherwise, I'll claw my face right off, which would not fall under appropriate things to do in front of a potential bedmate.

"Katie!"

Both our heads swivel in the direction of the voice. My sister weaves through the crowd, her eyes locked on the woman next to me.

"There you are." Tracy stops in front of me and loops her arm through the woman's as alarm bells echo in my head.

Katie?

"I really hope you two made up, because I want to make this party an annual thing, and I have to have my two favorite people here." Tracy squeezes her arm, then turns to me and gasps. "Oh my God, what happened to your face?"

The mystery woman—or Katie, evidently—covers her mouth, but it could easily be because of the monumental mistake we've made.

I kissed the woman I stood up last night.

Fuck.

How is this happening?

I give in to the burning urge on my face and scratch my cheek, digging what short fingernails I have into my skin with the sole mission of satisfying this itch.

This can't be happening.

As I stare at Katie, I'm more dumbfounded than the first time I saw a subway map.

Tracy yanks on my hand, forcing me to face her. "You're having an allergic reaction. Did you bring Benadryl?" She pushes me to sit on the bench in the entryway by the front door. "Actually, I have some in my bathroom. I always keep it on hand. Hang tight."

Tracy continues mumbling under her breath as she races down the hall, her feet sweeping across the wooden floor in frenzied steps.

Katie approaches right as my sister returns, holding a pink box high above her head like a prize. "Here you go," she announces and hands me a small pill. "Wait. Does anyone have water?"

"I'll get some," Katie offers quietly from behind her, but another woman steps forward with a full glass.

I take the medicine while most of the guests now stare at me. As if the audience itself isn't bad enough, water dribbles down my chin due to the swelling.

This is fucking humiliating.

"How the hell did this happen? You're only allergic to cinnamon, and I'm always so careful about keeping it out of the house. I even told everyone not to bring anything with it tonight, but I know it can be hard to remember, especially during this time of year." Tracy chews on her bottom lip, her eyes darting between mine in search of answers.

"Oh my God" sounds a whisper from behind her.

We both look up to find Katie's mouth hanging open. A mixture of shock and guilt masks her previously radiant features, and her already light complexion turns paler.

"I brought, um, apple cookies. I didn't... know," she stutters. "I decided at the last minute to come, and I... I didn't know."

"I didn't eat any, though," I say slowly, but my heart beats wildly, throbbing in my head like a hammer.

Katie bites her bottom lip and averts her gaze. "Well, I ate a couple right before…"

"Why would that matter? You would've had to—" Tracy's widening eyes bounce between us, and she shoots upright from her kneeled position in front of me.

The rest of the party seems to have gotten back to their conversations, obviously bored with our predicament.

But the three of us are just getting started.

"You *kissed* him?" she asks Katie, then whirls around to me so fast her hair gets caught in her gaping mouth. "You kissed her? When? How?"

"I'm so sorry. I didn't mean for any of this to happen. I was—"

Pushing off the bench to stand, I hiss, "Did you do this on purpose to get back at me?"

"What? No!" She clutches her chest like it's the most ridiculous thing she's ever heard.

But I know better. Nothing is off the table when it comes to lovers' quarrels, as I've seen in my profession plenty of times.

One scorned wife purposely gave her cheating husband undercooked chicken. A jealous husband told his apathetic wife they were going out to eat, but he ended up pushing her out of the car before they ever reached the restaurant. The latter was all because she refused to acknowledge his new shirt, which he'd bought specifically to impress her.

There's no such thing as going too far when it comes to matters of the heart, so I wouldn't put it past Katie to execute this kind of revenge for standing her up last night.

"I didn't even know who you were, let alone that you had

a cinnamon allergy," she insists. "I didn't think we'd end up kissing before we learned each other's names, either."

"I can't believe this," Tracy chimes in.

"What I can't believe is your little story." I pin Katie under my searing glare. "I stood you up, but I'm not sorry. I knew there was something up with you, and this just fucking proves it."

Tracy places a hand on my chest. "Whoa, whoa—"

"You know what?" Katie eases Tracy out of the way and steps in front of me, squaring her shoulders. Any signs of remorse have evaporated, and in its place is assertiveness. "I'm glad you didn't show up for our date. It would've been a total waste of time, so thank you for doing me that favor."

"The pleasure was all mine," I sneer, anxious for this medicine to kick in already, but I know it's going to take at least another twenty minutes.

I haven't had a reaction in years, and I forgot how uncomfortable even a mild one like this can be. It doesn't make me feel better to have a bunch of strangers staring at me once again, either.

How could I have been so trusting so quickly? If my fucking hormones hadn't gotten in the way, I would've practiced more caution. I study produce at the grocery store more carefully than I did this woman before I kissed her under the mistletoe.

She was just too captivating. Too easy to lose myself in. Our conversation was natural, and I was actually enjoying myself.

Before it all came crashing down on me like the debris of a bursting Christmas pinata.

An audience gathers, new interest ignited in our tiff, and my hives could very well be from embarrassment now, instead of the reaction.

"There's nothing to see here," Tracy tells her guests as she ushers Katie and me toward the stairs, where she moves the elves out of the way and clears a path for us to climb up. "Let's get you two alone."

"I don't want to be alone with *her*," I spit due to my distaste for Katie or my reaction. It could go either way.

"Right. Because being alone with you is exactly how I wanted to spend my evening," Katie deadpans.

Tracy shoves us into her bedroom and slams the door shut.

Katie's headband teeters off her head as she huffs and puffs. After fumbling with it for a few comical seconds—much to my delight—she yanks it off and sticks her pointer finger in my face. "You are a lying, egotistical—"

"Me? What about you? You're a petty woman—"

"—asshole with intimacy and commitment issues—"

"—who's supposed to be helping teenagers, not filling them with filthy ideas of sexuality."

She drops her arm to her side and steps back, her mouth frozen in a shocked *O*.

Beside her, Tracy slinks backward too and wraps her arms around her midsection.

"Is that why you didn't show up last night?" Katie asks. "Because of what they're saying about me?"

"It's because of what you haven't said. Mainly, an apology." I take a deep breath in an attempt to slow my rapid heart rate, but it doesn't help.

Her crestfallen expression gnaws at me.

And when she laughs so humorlessly, the sting grows far more vicious.

She doesn't resemble the woman who's enchanted me all night. Instead, she instantly becomes only a shell of herself, and my mind plays tricks on me, further confusing any logic I thought I had.

But my throat is too clogged to speak out. To say something to coax her vibrant confidence back to the forefront, even though I don't regret what I said. I just regret being the one to cause such damn devastation in her eyes.

Katie turns her teary gaze toward my sister. "Thank you for, um, inviting me tonight," she whispers, then jerks the door open and disappears, her shoulders slumped and a metaphorical tail tucked between her legs.

Once we're alone, I stuff my hands into the pockets of my slacks and blow out a rough exhale. "Listen, Trace, I didn't know—"

"What happened to you?" She frowns. "Since when did you become such a cold-hearted dick?"

"What?" I hold up my hands. "I told you I didn't want to get involved with any scandals right now. You know I can't put my job on the line. It's bad for business."

"Is this *job* the only thing you care about? Because it's starting to look that way, and I've got to be honest—it's not my favorite look of yours." She scoffs, and I can practically feel an ulcer burning through my stomach. "This city and your *super* important clients seem to have turned you into a whole new person. Small-town, Kansas Griffin never would've done or said the things you have in the last two days."

I barely flinch at the mention of my roots. I've done everything possible to adapt and integrate myself into the tapestry of this shameless fucking city, and I'm not going to let a guilt trip take everything away.

Tracy's only lived here for less than four months. She has yet to find out just how royally this cut-throat city can chew people like us up and spit us out if we don't tread carefully.

Besides, she doesn't have all the facts. Tracy—and Katie, for that matter—have no idea just how involved I am with this mess. Otherwise, they wouldn't give me such shit.

Silently, my sister leaves me alone with the war between my head and chest.

And somewhere between it all is the taste of Katie.

She excited me. For the first time in months—maybe, ever—my heart rate sped up for reasons other than a hard workout at the gym.

But it was all a ruse. It was the work of a devious temptress.

And it would be in my best interest to forget our damn kiss.

CHAPTER
Four

KATIE

"I ALMOST KILLED HIM."

Erin nearly spits out her soy latte.

"I accidentally licked cinnamon into his mouth, and he's incredibly allergic," I lament as dramatically as the students did in the Shakespeare play a couple years ago.

But this situation totally warrants grief, for many reasons.

Across the table, Erin grimaces. "I have so many questions. First of all, is he okay? And second, why did you phrase it like that?"

"He's fine." I take a sip of my own coffee and relent, "And okay, I could've phrased it differently. Noted."

Staring out the window, I lap up the foam from my bottom lip and sigh. Normally, she and I sit in one of our classrooms, or the teachers' lounge, while we gossip. We drink Keurig coffee from one of the three mugs in our rotation as we chat and laugh over Karen's or Nancy's antic of the week.

But as of today, we're officially out on Christmas break.

We should be celebrating with happy hour like we did last year, but I'm not in the mood. Not with everything going on.

So, instead, we're meeting at a coffee shop to gossip over barista-brewed coffee served in plastic cups with our names on the sides.

I twist the cup in my hand, my lip twitching in delight over the cute snowflakes floating across the side. It's my favorite time of year—a break from the stress of school for the best holiday of all—and I'm sulking.

It's not because I already miss the stuffy teachers' lounge, either.

I still haven't even finished decorating my apartment. Given how small it is, it should be an easy afternoon's job, but I can't muster enough holiday cheer.

I didn't mope this hard when they canceled my TV show as a kid. Of course, at the time, I was more concerned about riding my bicycle faster than my friend Beverly or learning to paint with my neighbor, who often babysat me. To me, those things held more weight than my show, but my mom was devastated. In turn, I was crushed on her behalf.

I hated being in the limelight then, and it was just a cute children's show about bees. It was nothing like this current media frenzy. If they find out about *Little Miss Bumble's Bees*, I dread the criticism and rumors they'll concoct out of a short and innocent Hollywood career.

"What exactly happened?" Erin squeezes my hand in encouragement. She's been doing a lot of that over the last few weeks. I don't know how she finds the strength, but I hope to God she doesn't lose it—for her sake and mine. It's part of her charm.

"I kissed Griffin, and it's how I almost killed him," I answer more clearly.

"I missed one hell of a party, didn't I?" she teases, and it puts me at ease enough to laugh.

I tell my friend the whole story, speaking in complete, coherent sentences for the first time since we sat down.

Who can blame me, though?

It's been hard to think straight since my life has been turned upside down, and Griffin threw me for yet another loop at the party.

His coffee-colored hair matched his eyes. The charcoal suit he wore looked as flawless as it did expensive, and the smolder he flashed right before he took me in his arms for our kiss sent me into another dimension.

Then he snatched the single shred of dignity I had and destroyed it with only a few words.

"He suggested *I* should be the one to apologize. Can you believe him?" I sit back in my chair with a huff. "I wish I wouldn't have walked away. I should've stood my ground. I mean, I was already on a roll with my comebacks. I should've thrown one last punch and wiped the stupid smirk off his handsome face."

"Why didn't you?"

"Because I was too dazed from his kiss," I blurt and squeeze my eyes closed, but it does nothing to ward off the shame consuming my entire body.

Why can't I stop thinking about Griffin's damn lips on mine?

He kissed me like a hungry man. His grip on me was firm and passionate, and his tongue was skilled. It felt so good and right and perfect.

When he pulled back, all I kept wondering was what else his tongue and fingers could do.

Then there was the hardening tent between his legs.

By the end of our smoking hot kiss, I could feel the tip of him against my lower stomach, and if we'd been at my own house, I would've nudged us toward my bedroom and ripped his pants off.

After I learned who he was, the fantasy shattered faster than a bat colliding with a glass window.

Too bad no glass ceilings are being shattered with my art show.

If it hadn't been for the "scandal," Griffin would've showed up to our blind date, we might've even gone to Tracy's party together, and we could have avoided this drama entirely.

What-ifs are futile, though. The reality is that the art show did happen. Horace is suing me. And I kissed my best friend's brother on a whim, all because of a stupid feeling in my belly and a cursed piece of mistletoe.

"I should hate him," I say on a laugh, but it comes out as more of a scoff.

"Our hearts—and hormones—never know the difference between what we should or shouldn't want. They just know what feels right."

"Did you read that on a fortune cookie?" I narrow my eyes at my genuine but very cooky friend.

"Nope. That was purely Erin Hayes at your service." She takes a minibow, curling herself into the motion on her seat. She's petite and flexible enough to make the movement look natural, even.

Shaking my head, my smile lingers, but I'm no closer to finding my inner balance or zen—or whatever the hell Erin calls it. "I was supposed to claim my coal and have fun, like my mother insists of me every chance she gets, but look where it's gotten me."

"Maybe you're looking at this all wrong. What if this is your opportunity to change a cynic's mind? You could alter Griffin's perspective, and from there, maybe the rest of Manhattan will follow."

"So, what you're telling me is that I'm in a completely impossible situation." I groan, exuding doubt with every exhale. "You didn't see him, Erin. He was so adamant about being right. I don't think divine intervention would do me any good where he's concerned."

"There's no such thing as impossible, unless you're talking about changing history—now that can't be undone."

"Thanks," I say sarcastically, but she pulls yet another light giggle from me. I think the woman has actual magical powers. "Just promise me one thing. Make sure your principal boyfriend doesn't fire me, please."

Since she's dating our boss, I thought it was a fair shot.

"You know Oliver respects and supports you. He has not acted otherwise, but unfortunately, there's a board to sway too."

"I'm right to worry, aren't I?"

She vehemently shakes her head and purses her lips. "This isn't over, and the whole faculty and I are behind you. We're in this together. If they attack you, they attack us all."

"Thank you. I don't know how I'd survive all this without you."

"I've got you," she reassures me, and I believe her. "What is your mother saying about all this?"

I take a deep breath to steel myself in the same way I do when I feel a chill coming on. "She is furious on my behalf, which she showed by advising me that the best damage control for my public image is hiring the greatest lawyer and adopting a sick poodle." I roll my eyes, and next to my half-empty coffee cup, my phone buzzes with an incoming call. With one glimpse at the name on my screen, my jaw drops. "It's Tommy."

There's a chill, all right.

"Really? When was the last time he called?"

"Almost two months ago when he dumped me," I grind out, then scoop the vibrating phone up to answer.

"I'm going to use the restroom," Erin whispers, hooking her thumb over her shoulder.

I stare after her as she maneuvers through the crowded

counter. Some patrons wait not so patiently for their orders, folding their arms across their chests and shooting glares toward the baristas. Others text on their phones like they have nowhere else to be this morning. I'm in the latter category, but none of them appear as overwhelmed as me.

"Um, hey" is the first thing out of Tommy's mouth.

"Did you mean to call me?" I ask, caution front and center.

"Yes."

After a tense pause, I press, "What's up, Tommy?"

"Have you, um, seen the latest article floating around?"

"What are you talking about?"

He audibly inhales, but I don't hear him release it.

He's holding his breath.

This can't be good.

Finally, he speaks up again. "It's about... you and me."

My heart sinks into my stomach as I shoot upright in my seat.

"They're saying you have a history of unethical behavior, Katie," he says, and his words emit a host of sympathy and discomfort. He obviously hates being the messenger of such news, and I have to appreciate his willingness to check in, even though I detest what he's saying.

"Oh my God," I whisper, leaning my head forward until my flushed skin hits the cool wood of the table.

"They reached out to me for a comment last week, but I refused, obviously. I didn't think they had enough to actually release the story, so I didn't say anything. But, it's out there."

Harsh headline possibilities further disgracing my character dash through my mind. Tears sting my eyes and threaten to spill, so I keep my head down and hidden. The media would just love a public breakdown, wouldn't they?

"I'm sorry, Katie." He sounds genuine. Although it's a kind sentiment, it only fuels my urge to cry. "Is there anything I can do?"

I bite my lip and tilt my head back far enough to keep the

tears at bay. "Actually, yes. Send me the link to the article, please."

"Are you sure? Because it says some other things."

"What other things?" I take a deep breath. "It doesn't matter. Please just send it."

Once my phone buzzes with his text, I thank him and end the call.

Tommy's kindness is what drew me to him in the first place. That, and he's as hot as a steaming cup of apple cider. As sweet and tangy too.

But his honest and kind heart is what kept me invested. It's why I refused to give up on him while we went out. I knew from the start that he wasn't ready for anything serious, so I agreed to something fun.

Besides, my mom's been in my ear about keeping my distance from committed romantic involvements—or entanglements, as she refers to them. I adopted such an attitude somewhere along the many cautionary tales she preached like a sermon.

When Tommy and I ran into each other outside of school and hit it off, his divorce had just been finalized. I should've known what havoc such an experience would wreak on a person. After all, I've lived it through my mother, but I was too stubborn to accept the reality.

A few weeks into our casual relationship, Tommy ended things. I would've been more heartbroken had we slept together, but we'd only been out a few times. Most of our dates—if I can even call them that—included him ranting about his ex-wife while I ordered one glass of wine after the next.

It was for the best, and we're even making our way toward friendship. We clearly care about each other if he's calling to warn me about the latest news of my backward spiral into fame.

And I could use as many friends as possible right about now.

"What's that look for?" Erin slides back into her seat, her concerned but empathetic once-over boring into me with the force of a hundred hugs. "Did Tommy upset you?"

"Yes, but it's not what you think." I skim the article he sent, using a trembling finger to scroll up and down the phone screen. "There's a new article out, and they're making me out to be a whore. Well, they were doing that before, but they spread my supposed indiscretions over a wider variety."

She gasps and leans forward for a better look. "What does it say exactly?"

"Oh my God." I freeze with my mouth agape as I get to an especially degrading part. It must be the "other things" Tommy mentioned. "They're claiming I show a pattern of scandalous behavior like I'm some nympho. In addition to exposing my relationship with Tommy, the jackass writer of this article says I had a secret affair with the new principal at our school."

"No!" She gasps again, but it's louder and more offended this time, presumably since she's involved in the ludicrous slander now. "But I'm the one who's dating Oliver, not you."

"I'm aware," I say sarcastically, my stomach shriveling up with nervous tension. "Why can't you be the one getting sued instead of me?" I look up from my phone with a frown. "Shit. I'm so sorry. I don't mean it. I'm actually happy for you and Oliver, but I'm really freaking sad for me."

The saint of a woman squeezes my hand again. "I'm so sorry, Katie."

I groan and click my phone off, my sullen eyes reflecting back at me from the dark screen.

This is rock bottom, isn't it?

There have to be juicier stories than mine out there. This is New York, after all. There are tons of more exciting things happening around here. Yet, the vultures have latched on to me.

Sighing, I push my cup away, suddenly not in the mood for anything other than a large glass of wallowing. "Can you use your crystal ball or whatever to tell me what the future holds? Please tell me it gets better."

"No crystal ball." Her encouraging smile transforms into one of amusement as she says, "I can ask my Ouija board, though."

A soft but humorless laugh escapes under my breath.

"I wouldn't give up on claiming your coal just yet. You can still have fun this holiday season and shake things up." She leans back in her chair, completely relaxed, and I wish I had an ounce of her confidence. "I mean, you and I both know this lawsuit doesn't have even a pinky toe to stand on. Oliver isn't going to fire you, and even though the board is staying far too quiet and hesitant, they know they can't afford to lose you. You're too great at your job, which is why they didn't immediately fire you. Plus, you're a badass, with killer heels in your closet. Take them out for a spin tonight, and forget the last month."

I find myself nodding along with her, but I'm not sold. "Claiming my coal has been biting me in the ass, Erin. Let's see…" I hold my finger up and tick off each item on my own naughty list. "This lawsuit may keep me from entering the school premises, and Oliver may not have a choice but to fire me, depending on what the board has to say. Let's face it—they might not be able to afford to lose me, but the scandal might become a much bigger risk. My lawyer is proving to be useless. I haven't spoken to him since last week, and I have no idea if he's working on my case at all. And the guy I kissed under the mistletoe like my life depended on it turned out to be a giant jerk. Living on the edge hasn't been working out for me, wouldn't you agree?"

"Yeah," she draws out. "You probably should've just

watched Hollie Berry and Ian Brock in *All Snowed Inn* instead of trying to follow her lead in reality."

I let out an exasperated huff. "Exactly."

"You did have fun, though, right?" she chirps.

My friend is relentless, that's for sure, and I can't help but smile. After all, she's not wrong. I have had fun, and I don't regret my actions.

Except for the kiss, anyway, but even that was mind-blowing. Truth be told, I wouldn't take back the actual kiss, but if was gifted a do-over, I'd just run away the second it ended to avoid the hellacious aftermath.

"Hollie Berry had fun too, if her pictures from Vegas were any indication, but she hasn't shown her face in public since the interview. Even though she did nothing wrong—just as I didn't, either. But we're the ones hiding while our names are dragged through the dirty, dirty mud."

Erin hums in response, her face crestfallen, and it's how I feel times a million.

There's nothing to say, anyway. She can't help me.

Hell, her boyfriend, the principal of the school, can't help me. My professional fate is not entirely up to him. If it were, I'd sleep a lot better at night.

But the reality is that I'm on my own in every sense.

No lawyer.

No boyfriend.

No naughty delight.

Merry freaking Christmas to me.

CHAPTER
Five

KATIE

I STROLL along the sidewalk past a couple with shopping bags loaded onto their arms like I do with my grocery bags just so I don't have to make multiple trips to and from my apartment. It makes me smile, but it's quickly wiped away as a sharp gust of wind slaps my cheek. I squeeze my eyes closed against it, and when I open them again, I wish I hadn't.

Because what I see makes my damn heart sink.

I should've stayed home, but Tracy called. I couldn't *not* come running. She just hadn't said her brother would be here too.

"What're you doing here?" Griffin asks, closing the door to Tracy's brownstone behind him. His wide stance is intimidating, but that's not what steals my breath.

Griffin's wavy hair is tousled to the side, revealing deep brown eyes and red-tinted cheekbones like he's sunburned. It rounds his rigid edges into something softer. More accessible. Less hostile.

It makes me wish on every one of Erin's precious stars that things were different between us.

His scowling eyes still make the hair at the back of my neck stand, but I tilt my chin up and refuse to let him affect me. "I'm coming to see Tracy. She is my friend, after all."

"Well, she's my sister."

"Okay," I draw out, matching his exasperated tone with my own. "Are we about to fight over custody of her?"

"Of course not. That would be ridiculous." He scoffs and places his hands on both hips, standing his ground in front of the door.

I take the last step and stop an inch away from him, the notes of his cologne bringing with them memories of the party last weekend.

The way his spicy smell filled my senses when he leaned in to cover my mouth with his.

The faint, upbeat melody of Christmas music slowing down as time stood still while he kissed me.

I grind my teeth, resenting how freaking good he smells. How sleek and handsome he is in his navy suit, tucked away beneath a long peacoat.

Griffin was made for this look. Judging by appearances alone, he belongs on the cover of a business magazine, or the next issue of *People*'s Sexiest Man Alive.

What would he look like in a T-shirt and jeans? Or plaid pajamas? I bet he'd wear those well too.

But unfortunately, no matter how sexy he is in any type of clothing, his pompous attitude would still ruin his appeal.

"How long are you going to block the door? Because I'm on break, so I have nowhere to be. I can literally stand here all afternoon if I need to." I fold my arms over my chest, containing my body heat against the winter chill—and his steely gaze.

"I'm off work and finished with the last of my Christmas shopping, so I, too, have all afternoon." He locks his eyes on mine like we've entered a staring contest.

"Add *petty* to the list of things wrong with you," I snap.

"Add *annoyingly immature* to the list of your nuisances."

"You look exactly like the douchey ex-boyfriend in every Hallmark movie."

"You're the captain of the ship sailing straight for Crazy City."

The door swings open, and we both fling our gazes at a wide-eyed Tracy. "What are you two doing?" she hisses, glancing around the neighborhood.

I turn back to Griffin, my heavy breaths releasing in hot, foggy puffs as I realize how close we're standing.

The lips I've dreamed about for days are only an inch away.

They're teasing and frustrating and kissable.

I've officially lost my mind.

"I was just leaving, and so was Katie," he clips.

"*Katie* just got here," I shoot back, punctuating each word with added flare, and it easily gets his attention. "You're the one who won't let me in."

"Both of you get in here before you embarrass me so badly I have to cut my lease short and move." Tracy yanks on our arms to pull us inside, but neither of us goes willingly.

The second my hand accidentally brushes against Griffin's, I jerk away and mutter angry words. I receive a few curses under his breath in response.

Once the door is closed to the outside world, warmth relieves us of the New York winter, but it's hard to revel in it with this tension blasting us into a realm of discomfort—and it's definitely about to get worse.

Tracy throws her hands up. "What is the matter with y'all?"

"Careful—your Kansas is showing." Her arrogant and frustratingly sexy brother smirks.

"And your asshole is showing." She pins him under her murderous glare while I stifle a snicker.

STUCK UNDER THE MISTLETOE

He grinds his jaw, audibly working his teeth back and forth against each other.

I tilt my head, raising my eyebrows to say *ha-ha, you're in trouble*, but my victory is short-lived.

"And you." Tracy turns her annoyed expression toward me. "I thought you were better than to let some pretentious New Yorker get under your skin."

In my periphery, I see Griffin puff out his chest. Then I catch the exact moment he realizes she didn't exactly give him a compliment.

"Hey!" He holds his hands out to his sides. "Whose side are you on?"

"Neither—obviously. You're both acting like children." She lets out an irritated exhale. "Now, what am I going to do with *y'all*? We have to figure something out, so we can all get along like grown-ups. When I moved out here, I was so excited for my new job, but above all, I was happy to finally be close to the two people I love most. I can't stand the thought of you two fighting all the time."

During a heavy pause, I keep my eyes trained on the Santa wearing sunglasses on Tracy's wall. I definitely try not to think about the last time Griffin and I were both here. The night we shared a kiss under the same mistletoe that stares at us now from above our heads.

Finally, Griffin the Grinch breaks the silence. "You love us more than Mom and Dad? Can't wait to break it to them when they visit next week."

"Out." Tracy shoves him toward the door.

"I was kidding." He only skids a couple inches backward, given how hard he is to budge. "I'm sorry, okay? I'll behave."

"No. I need you out. I can't deal with this right now because I have a date with my neighbor, and I'm not going to let you two make me late." She continues nudging him toward the door and looks over her shoulder at me. "Did you bring the earrings I asked for?"

"Of course. That's why I'm here." I give her a tight-lipped smile as she opens the door and pushes Griffin out of it.

"Wait, you have a date? Who's your neighbor?" He turns from side to side, seemingly hoping for a glimpse.

"His name is Evan. He's a contractor, and he's the hottest guy I've ever seen. Which is why I'm kicking you out." Tracy marches back inside, grabs the earrings from me, and tugs me toward the door. "You're out too."

"What? Why me?" I swat at her grip on my arm.

"Here's twenty-five dollars. Now, shoo." She slaps a couple bills into my palm and retreats into the toasty side of the threshold.

"You're paying us to leave?" Griffin asks with a scoff.

"No." She smiles. "I'm paying you to go get a falafel and work your shit out. I'm hosting a New Year's Eve party, and I don't want you two fighting over the champagne."

"Another party? Since when did you become such a popular hostess?"

"People change. Sometimes for better"—she points to herself, then jabs her forefinger into Griffin's chest—"and sometimes for worse."

She slams the door shut, leaving Griffin and me dumbfounded on her stoop.

"What the hell?" He spins in place, tilting his head back. "This is your fault. Before you, she laughed at all my jokes, and she never would've thrown me out on my ass like this."

I roll my eyes and take off down the steps until I reach the sidewalk, where I march down to the crosswalk.

"Where are you going?" the Scrooge calls from behind me, and the sound of his footsteps grows louder as he approaches.

While we wait for the light to turn, I hold up the money. "To get a falafel." I state the obvious. It's what his sister suggested, and no matter how much I despise this man, I love his sister more. I'd do anything for her, including trying to make peace with Griffin Chase.

"Those fried balls of grease from a food truck are so bad for you. You're just asking for a stomachache."

"You don't have to join me," I shoot back as the last car darts down the street, clearing the way for us to cross.

Again, I hear him coming up behind me. "So, you're not proposing we work our shit out, then?"

"I'm not *not* proposing it, but it's your choice. I'm not your keeper, and neither is Tracy."

It takes a few blocks to find a food truck, as most hibernate in the winter. But one finally comes into view, and I halt in front of it, the strong herbs and smell of onion wafting over me and reminding me just how hungry I am. I place my order without needing to look at the menu, then turn to Griffin in question.

He takes the hint and adds his own order—a chicken and rice bowl without sauce.

I laugh under my breath over his boring request, and he tosses me a glare.

Once we have our food, I make my way toward the quaint park on the corner. It's too cold to enjoy a nice day outside, so it's relatively deserted, much to my dismay. Judging from how the last two conversations with Griffin have gone, I might need witnesses.

Seated on an ass-numbingly cold bench, I steal a peek at his profile and the harsh cut of his diamond-shaped jaw. In contrast is the playful curve of the tip of his nose and the endearing red tint at the top of his ear.

As he dips his head down, he studies his food like he's afraid to eat it. I have no problem digging into my own, though.

When I studied abroad in France during college, I got used to trying different foods. I couldn't understand most of the things on any menu in front of me, so I had to become adventurous with my diet.

I only had one bad experience with a bite of escargot, but I believe I'm better for it now.

After I'm done swallowing a delicious bite of my "fried balls of grease," I break the silence. "Are you going to tell me why you blocked my way into your sister's house and landed us here in detention?"

"No." He sighs and lifts his head again, resigned. It's either because he decides he's not going to eat, or he's finally going to meet me halfway. "Maybe."

"I'll be here for another ten minutes, so decide quickly."

"I thought you didn't have anywhere to be."

"I don't. I say that because it'll take me ten minutes, at most, to finish my food and go home, where it's nice and warm." I pop another bite into my mouth and chew obnoxiously for his benefit as the cold chill nips at my cheeks and flings my hair over my shoulders.

I'm sure the strands are thoroughly tangled over the hood of my coat, but that's a future problem between my brush and me.

He leans against the back of the bench and angles his body toward mine, shifting so much the Styrofoam box in his lap squeaks like a chew toy. "Did you really have an affair with your new boss?"

"What?" Bits of falafel fly out of my mouth, while the other half of my bite nearly chokes me.

Instead of cheering for my downfall, as part of me suspected he would, my nemesis pats me on the back.

Once my throat is free of all debris, I take a deep breath, careful not to choke on the frigid air.

"You read the latest article of my supposed scandal, huh?" I croak, wiping my chin with a napkin he gives me. Should I assume it's an olive branch?

"I did." He rubs his hands down his slacks. "I wasn't

checking up on you or anything. It was forwarded to me by a friend. Miles is turning into a major gossip. We went out for a beer—because, contrary to what my sister thinks, I do enjoy time outside of the office—but none of that is important, anyway."

Is Griffin… rambling?

Wow. Mr. Serious and Super Judgmental is nervously babbling, and it raises his factor of adorable to another level.

"I didn't think you were checking up on me," I offer. An amused smile tugs at my lips as I tease, "I do now."

He shakes his head. "Forget I asked. It's none of my business."

"I didn't."

"What?" He snaps his head up.

"I never dated my boss. A friend and coworker did—is. They're still dating, and they're really solid." My grin turns wistful. "Erin and Oliver, our principal, are in love."

The longer Griffin stares blankly at me, the more uncomfortable I become. Did I say too much? Why is he looking at me like that?

I mean, I just stated the facts to answer his question, but the way he's watching me is more similar to how one might admire the Christmas tree at Rockefeller Center, not a stigmatized art teacher.

My phone buzzes in my coat pocket, jarring us out of this weird trance, and I'm disappointed. As soon as I see my lawyer's name on the screen, I tell Griffin, "Sorry, but I have to take this."

I set my food down and stand, bringing the phone to my ear to answer. We're two words past the greeting, and I wish I would've declined the call.

"Are you drunk?" I screech into the phone.

"I'm at a bar with some buddies for a little fun. Why don't you join us? You're the kind of girl who likes to party, am I right?"

I cringe at the slimy insinuation in his voice. Is this guy for real?

As he laughs over a few more disgusting suggestions with whom I assume are his "buddies," my restraint snaps. "Listen, asshole, I thought you were calling about my case, but forget it. You're fired, and I don't want to hear from you again, you son of a—"

Before I can finish laying into him, the phone is ripped away from me.

Griffin snatches it and roars into the speaker. "I don't know who this is, but if you contact Ms. Bumble again or cause her any distress, you'll be hearing from me regarding harassment and exploitation suits."

He pauses, and I stand frozen next to him, my vision turning a whimsical shade of pink in much the same way cartoons change colors when they're seeing someone in a new light.

Griffin is standing up for me.

And he's damn sexy doing so too.

His hair bounces to the side in the wind, and he ruffles it up with his large free hand as he spins in place, anger rolling off him in waves. As he scolds the scum on the other end, an accent I've never heard from him drips from each word. There's suddenly a Midwestern twang in it, which grows thicker the longer he's on the phone, and it gives me butterflies.

Who is this man?

"Shut up," he says into the phone. "Stop fucking talking and learn a thing or two about how to treat a woman. Never disrespect her. If I hear you've even breathed in her direction, I'll send you right back to your hometown of Hell. In the meantime, I'll be in touch regarding a restraining order."

He pushes his thumb against the screen to end the call with such force that I'm surprised the screen is still intact.

Truthfully, I'm surprised he doesn't burst into a thousand pieces from the rage reeling off his tense shoulders.

I gulp as he turns to hand me back my phone. "Um…" My voice catches on the lump in my throat.

"He won't be bothering you anymore," he says semi-evenly and smooths his hair over to one side, his neck sporting blotches of crimson wrath.

"Thank you," I whisper as he walks back to the bench and takes a seat. I'm right behind him, and my confidence grows with each step I take toward him—as does the heat in my core.

I mean, that may have been the sexiest thing any guy has ever done for me.

"Thank you," I repeat, but it's louder this time as I return to my spot beside him.

"I didn't do anything special," he bites out. For once, his aggravation isn't directed toward me.

"You didn't even know what he said to me before you grabbed the phone."

"I knew enough from the change in your expression." Griffin turns toward me. "You normally have this… spark in your eyes. You're confident, which is one of the things that drew me to you at the Christmas party. And even though you sounded like you could probably hold your own, I hated the way that spark disappeared."

My lips part, and the intensity in his dark eyes makes me squirm.

Griffin Chase just gave me a compliment.

With proud tears stinging the backs of my eyes, I manage, "Lately, it feels like people have just been looking for ways to knock me down. It's nice for someone to stick up for me for a change."

He clenches his jaw as he watches me, curiosity and something else floating in the depths of his rich amber eyes. Is it remorse?

"You did catch me off guard, though. I never would've expected you to jump to my rescue." I laugh, but it's cut off by the stern glare he shoots my way.

"I might not know exactly what the animal said to you on the phone, but after talking to him for a second, I can gather the gist." He leans forward, and I'm transfixed by the passion masking any other emotion I caught before. "No matter what's happened, there's no fucking way I'd let any bastard treat you so disparagingly. Contrary to what you might believe, Katie, I'm not a monster."

My sleazy lawyer—ex-lawyer, actually—struck a nerve, and I'm seeing a whole new, honorable side to Griffin.

In fact, it's hard to believe this is the same guy who stood me up for our date and lashed out at me after our kiss.

But he did.

He did those things, and it stings now more than ever.

What am I thinking getting caught up in his heroic side? It's not who he really is.

Griffin might not be a monster, but he still thinks I am.

"A rose for your beautiful wife?" We both turn to find a woman holding out a bright red flower, a wide ribbon tied around the stem, as she tilts her head from Griffin to me. There are several such roses in a small cart, which the woman holds steady with one gloved hand.

Her face is mostly covered by a thick scarf, and I realize I'm shivering. How long have we been sitting here? And how is my ass not frozen to the bench already?

Griffin's own face pales as his panicked gaze bounces from the woman to me and back to the rose. He's not frozen in place from the cold, either, but the misconception that we're together.

"*Excusez-moi, je ne comprends pas,*" I blurt and clutch my chest as I follow it up with a forced smile. "*Je suis désolé.*"

With an understanding nod, she rounds her cart and

pushes it back toward the sidewalk, leaving me, Griffin, and the awkward tension wrapped around us.

"What was that?"

I hop off the bench and slide my stiff hands into my pockets. "That was French I learned from my semester abroad."

"Impressive," he mutters, confusion still etched between his thick brows. "But it doesn't explain why—"

"I need to go." I swing my body around, practically forcing myself to leave him.

We made progress, right? We aren't yelling at each other anymore, which is all I was hoping for to begin with. I'm sure Tracy would agree that this was the best-case scenario, so it's safe for me to leave now without losing any more dignity—or pieces of my heart to this man.

"Katie! I can get you a damn rose," he calls out after me, and again, I hear his footsteps pounding on the pavement as he approaches.

The street blurs as tears of disappointment and humiliation fill my vision, so I pick up my pace. But I'm still not fast enough.

Griffin catches up to me and says, "I didn't show up to our date because the man who's suing you is one of my firm's long-time clients."

I halt.

The air is knocked out of me.

Of all the things I thought he'd say, this was not on my list of guesses.

Horace is his client? What the hell?

Slowly, I turn to face him again. He's standing with his hands in his pockets, and his posture isn't as confident as it's been each time we've crossed paths.

"I didn't want to get tangled up in the mess," he says, hanging his head.

"Why didn't you... tell me this from the beginning?" I sputter, my mind racing to fill in the gaps.

He holds his arms out, and a fraction of the previous tension dissipates. "Because I'm an asshole."

I blink.

A ghost of a smile flits across his lips. "I've gotten used to being an asshole, and I thought it was better to act as such, instead of being upfront and honest with you. It's also why I didn't call or text to at least tell you I wouldn't make it to dinner that night, and I should have. I should've... I should've done things differently, and I'm sorry."

I shake my head, squeezing my eyes closed. My heart thunders in my head as the loose gravel crunches beneath tires from someone crazy enough to ride their bicycle at this hour and in this cold weather.

"I mean, I wish I could argue with you, but you're very agreeable in your self-assessment."

"Thanks," he deadpans.

We lock eyes, and the sarcastic amusement slowly disappears from his expression.

His sharp jawline settles back into its usually clenched position, and his gaze roams over me, a plea marring his natural features.

I lick my lips and instinctively lean in, although I don't know what I'm hoping for. I don't know what we're doing or how he truly feels about me.

He might've finally explained his absence from our date, but does it change anything?

It does for me.

His admission of being an ass even makes me like him more.

As if our mistletoe kiss wasn't enough to make me goo for him, he goes and shows me how hot raw honesty can be.

Holy crap on a candy cane—I'm falling for Griffin Chase.

CHAPTER Six

GRIFFIN

"I'LL WALK you back to your place," I offer as Katie and I face each other, our breaths joining between us in a tiny cloud of confessions.

With all of our truth telling, I didn't realize how long we've been out here until the streetlamps blinked on and my ass started to freeze. I almost stuck to the frigid bench and became one with it.

Katie's cheeks are cranberry red, and her eyes have a gloss covering them like she's tearing up. The stinging wind has gotten the best of us both, as my own eyes water too. Aren't we a pair?

I place my hand on her lower back to lead her toward the road, throwing away the uneaten remnants of our food truck dinner on the way.

Christmas wreaths adorn the streetlamps we pass. White lights flicker to life, and people turn their house decorations on too. With each stoop we pass, it feels like more lights shine brightly beside us.

My heart flips as she glances over her shoulder back at

me. Her button nose is blushing a deeper cherry color than before, matching her cheeks, and her eyelashes flutter open and closed as she rests her chin on her shoulder. She's bundled up, but it's not enough to keep her warm.

My body hardens at the thought of being the one to heat her up.

To rip her puffy coat off and use her scarf to pull her toward me.

What's happening to me? I thought I'd decided I was through with her. Then Miles sent me the newest article, and I lost my damn head at the thought of her with other men.

It's why I had to ask. I even believed it would help me move on from our kiss if she were to tell me the article was true. That she dated the principal and the PE teacher.

But then she threw me off my axis and told me it's not true —the part about her boss, anyway.

And then the fucking tool on the phone made me see red. A violent red. Who the hell did he think he was to treat her with so little respect?

The need to protect her was overwhelming.

I hadn't felt such a powerful urge to be there for someone in a while. The dangerous thing is that I don't hate the satisfaction coursing through me from lending a hand.

For *her*.

"This is me." Katie stops in front of a white building crammed between two brown ones, a large window above the front door like it's standing guard.

"That was a quick walk." Over her shoulder, I can still see the park we left a couple blocks away.

She nods, and I don't miss the quick sweep of her gaze over my lips. It stirs something deep in my chest and reminds me of our kiss at the party.

It reminds me of how thrilling our instant chemistry was —and could be again.

"I live close to Tracy, which is how I was able to let her know of the available place she's currently renting."

"Very kind of you to help her out like that."

"I wouldn't be a good best friend if I didn't look out for her."

I teeter on my heels worse than if we were on a seesaw, and now, the weight has shifted to her.

It's up to Katie to ask me to come inside. To call an official truce.

Is that what I want, though?

I should leave, preferably before she says anything.

Because the way she's looking at me—like she *wants* to invite me inside—is too dangerous. I won't be able to say no, and until I can sort through my feelings, I shouldn't do anything rash.

"Thanks for walking me back." She starts to turn, and disappointment floods my body faster than a broken levee.

Before she sticks the key into the lock, I reach out. I don't know why, other than the slicing pain holding my heart hostage at the thought of leaving things between us like this. So lacking and cold.

It's not right.

The second my hand grips hers, she spins into my embrace and plants her lips on mine, and it *is* right.

Her kiss is surprising, and it knocks me off balance yet again. She's done so since the Christmas party, and just like our unforgettable kiss that night, this one sends an electric current throughout my body.

While the contact shocks me, it also relieves me, as if to say *fucking finally*.

"Want to come inside?" she murmurs against my lips as she arches her breasts into my chest.

I want to feel how hard her nipples are. How wet she is underneath. What pitch her moans are when she's being pleasured.

I want to be the one who makes her feel good.

I nod, and anticipation excites me as she unlocks the door and pulls me inside.

As soon as we step into her apartment, I press her against the closed door and devour her mouth, thrusting my tongue between her lips with avid determination to get my fill of this woman.

This sensational, funny, and sexy woman.

I would've missed out on this after I skipped our date. Had I missed the Christmas party too. The thought alone drives me to kiss her more feverishly.

My clumsy, eager hands finally find the zipper on her coat and tug it down to free her of the heaviest layer.

Between kisses, she stutters, "You're fucking hot when you're honest."

"Yeah?" I rasp against her swollen lips and shove my hand up her sweater until I find the edge of her bra. "How about we exchange a truth for every piece of clothing we lose?"

"I like the sound of that, but…"

"What?" I urge as I cup my hand over one silky fabric-covered breast.

"We need to hurry." She pants, then throws her coat the rest of the way off. "I hate brown gravy on my mashed potatoes, but I like white gravy on my biscuits."

I chuckle through my lust-filled fog as I shrug out of my coat and kick my shoes off. "I moved to New York City because my girlfriend dumped me while we were in college, and I wanted to show her what she was going to miss out on."

Katie's jaw drops, but I don't dwell. There's no time. I point to her sweater, hurrying her along as my stiffy becomes full-on painful. "I was the star of my own TV show as a kid called *Little Miss Bumble's Bees*," she says as her scarf flies over her head, then flutters to the ground by our feet.

"I definitely need to hear more about that." I drop my pants and step out of them, leaving a pool of expensive wool next to us. "I leave a light on while I sleep."

"I can't stop thinking about the cinnamon incident." She bites her lip as her mouthwatering breasts rise and fall with each labored breath. "It really was an accident, and I'm sorry. I even ripped any trace of cinnamon from this apartment—no plug-ins or spice in my cabinet. I left the windows open for three days straight to aerate this place, even though I didn't think you'd ever come here."

"I believe you, and I'm sorry I was such a dick afterward."

She nods her forgiveness and finally tears the sweater over her head, revealing the outlines of two perfectly curved breasts pushed toward each other with a red bra. Katie looks like an erotic gift on Christmas morning, and the urge to rip off the rest of her clothes like wrapping paper makes me crazy.

She makes me crazy and spontaneous and reckless.

My nostrils flare with impatience, but the timid shadow casting over her eyes stops me. "The picture I showcased from my art student was in honor of her mother, who has breast cancer, and it absolutely kills me that the media's shining such an ugly light on it."

This one makes my body freeze as I run my gaze over her. She's one surprise after another, isn't she? And the thought that I'll never be able to predict her excites me, even though I should probably be terrified.

Remaining still, my voice feels far away even to my own ears when I say, "I want kids someday."

"I've never been in love." She pulls her boots off, which land on the laminate floor with a thud. The sound echoes against my chest as her confession sinks in.

"That makes two of us," I admit as I unbutton the top of my shirt. I complete the simple task every day, but it's difficult right now. My fingers are trembling worse than when I took the bar.

"I haven't stopped thinking about our kiss since the night of the Christmas party." She peels her leggings down to her ankles and steps out of them with much more care than I did my own pants. She keeps her eyes on mine the entire time too.

"Another thing we have in common." I lick my lips and flick the last button on my shirt loose.

Before I can slide it off, she leaps into my arms, wraps her legs around my waist, and fuses her mouth with mine in a heated, sloppy, open-mouthed kiss.

She wants me as badly as I want her, and it's fucking sexy.

I carry her three steps to my left, nearly tumbling to my demise when my foot catches on her sweater. Quickly untangling myself from the thick material and without breaking our kiss, I set Katie on the nearest surface—the kitchen island.

Behind her, teal cabinets add splatters of color to the brown and cream backsplash. It's the best reflection of her.

I run my palm up her smooth thigh until I reach the silk of her panties. I ache to touch her everywhere.

To feel all of her.

She curves her back, pressing her breasts against my bare chest as she slides my shirt over both shoulders, leaving it haphazardly balanced on my upper arms.

"Take me," she whispers between moans and pants as I nip at the column of her throat, her hair wrapped in my fist at the nape of her neck. "Take me, Griffin."

I've never come so close to exploding as I do the second she writhes against me, her panty-clad heat begging for me. "There's nothing else I'd rather fucking do."

By some miracle, I find a condom in my wallet. I don't always carry them around anymore since I rarely date, but lucky for me, I stashed one in here the night of the Christmas party—ironically enough.

The ghost of mistletoes past came through for me, for sure.

As I sheath myself, my own touch and rubber causing my dick to twitch from being so achingly hard, Katie shifts to the edge of the island to remove her panties.

The second they fall from her feet, I nestle myself between her thighs and devour her plump lips. Shifting on the balls of my feet, I line myself up to her entrance and ease inside her tight channel.

Once I fill her, she drops her forehead to my shoulder, and her hot breath against my chest floats over my heart like it's knocking to be let in.

And fuck, do I want to open.

We shouldn't make sense. We shouldn't fit together so perfectly—in every sense—but we do.

And there's no going back now.

I grind my teeth and smooth her hair out of my mouth, then fist it again at the back of her head as I rock into her, her wetness coating my pulsing length.

So fucking sexy.

"Yes, Griffin. More of that." Her head rolls from side to side, then falls back as I slide deeper inside her, wave after wave of satisfaction washing over me with each thrust. "More," she repeats, placing both hands behind her to keep herself steady.

I grunt as I lean forward and bite the flesh above her bra, a feral need consuming me. I want to devour her.

I bring her hips dangerously close to the edge of the cool surface and fuck her harder, digging my fingers into the top of her ass.

The sound of her wetness dripping and coating me from the tip of my cock to my inner thighs, plus the sight of her tits bouncing so wildly, fuels me to pound into her like a madman.

And the volume of her seductive cries increases until her soft hums become overwhelming howls.

Spots fill my vision as an excruciatingly powerful release floods down between my legs, ready to burst.

I hold on with every ounce of self-control I can muster until she wails my name, her body quivering with her intense climax.

"Oh… shit…" She closes her eyes, then lets her head fall back again, the ends of her hair teasing the sink behind her.

"That's it, gorgeous." I beam as I peer down between us and growl with triumphant satisfaction when I glimpse my lower stomach glistening with her pleasure.

With metaphorical permission, my own release hits me, squeezing every bit of pent-up tension right out of my body. I collapse forward, resting my head between her breasts as I pump out the last of my climax.

She runs her fingers through my hair and holds me close as I fight for every breath.

"Not bad for the douchey ex-boyfriend from every Hallmark movie, huh?" I say hoarsely as I lean back to meet her shining gaze.

She laughs, and the exuberant sound fills me with more joy than I've ever experienced. Because that's what this was—an experience. It wasn't just sex or fun or an itch that needed scratching.

This was fucking real, and I need a repeat.

This woman is every bit as dangerous as I believed at first.

I wanted to take things slow and process what I feel for her, but my damn body took over, bringing my heart along with it.

The problem is that there are always consequences when mixing business and personal lives, and I most certainly am in deep trouble.

CHAPTER
Seven

KATIE

AFTER THE MAIN course of sex in the kitchen with a side of a delicious orgasm, Griffin helped me clean up and followed me to my bedroom.

I wouldn't have pegged him for a cuddler, but he's definitely good at it. He spoons me the same way I scoop up ice cream—like he means it.

The reassuring contact comforts me as I snuggle against his hard chest, warmed by him and the heavy comforter draped over us.

Tonight was the naughtiest I've ever been while sharing the truth.

"My calves are going to be sore tomorrow." He chuckles against the back of my head and places a kiss in my hair.

"Your calves?" I ask, confused over this topic shift as I intertwine my fingers through his and clutch our joined hands to my chest.

"They're going to be sore because I did a continuous calf raise while I fucked you," he whispers.

"My body thanks you," I say through a smile.

"You're trouble, aren't you?"

I turn in his arms to face him, committing everything about this night to memory. "I was going to say the same about you."

He kisses me, drawing my bottom lip between his teeth and nibbling on it like the full course wasn't enough, and he needs a snack.

It makes me grin against his mouth, and I can't help my giggle.

I don't know if I'll ever stop giggling.

This unexpected man makes me too giddy.

"We can talk about that. Or you could elaborate on this high school sweetheart of yours," I say, quirking a brow.

Griffin presses his forehead to mine, and it doesn't take long before he explains. It's obvious I've opened his floodgates, and I'm damn happy he's tearing down the wall he built between us.

"Her name was Megan. I asked her to prom in high school, and we were inseparable for almost four years. We went to the same college, which is where she met her now-husband. The asshole was her chemistry lab partner."

"Ouch."

"Yes, well, I showed her by moving to New York City, staying single, and making out with my sister's friends under the mistletoe," he teases.

"You mean there have been more?" I smack his chest, and my hand practically bounces off like a rubber ball against the chiseled surface.

"Nah. Just you." He kisses my forehead, and I instinctively close my eyes, melting into it.

"You said you've never been in love, but what about Megan? It sounds like you were heartbroken that she dumped you."

He stares over my head at the opposite wall, but I'm guessing it's not because I have a ridiculous cow painting hanging on it. It's the one tacky piece of art I have in this place—my version of a guilty pleasure.

Some have trashy TV and chocolate binges; I have a hot pink and black painting of a cow's face. I even named her Moo-lan.

No, the faraway look in Griffin's eyes is enough indication that he doesn't actually see it. "I loved Megan, but in hindsight, I wasn't *in* love with her. I cared deeply for her, but it just wasn't that life-upending feeling I imagine people have when they know they want to spend the rest of forever together. I've never come close to something like it. I've never even wanted to live with anyone."

"Never?"

He shrugs. "I almost asked a woman once. It was about three years ago, and right when I was going to ask, I had a gut reaction to run instead of finishing my question. So, I made up an excuse and bolted."

"Then what?"

"I took her out to dinner the next night and broke up with her." He gives me a tight-lipped smile. "What about you? Ever lived with anyone?"

"No."

"No PE teachers ever steal your heart?" He pokes my side and laughs, but there's something very real in his deep, darker-than-whiskey eyes.

"Smooth," I deadpan. "How long have you been keeping that question on the tip of your tongue?"

"Only since this afternoon," he soberly admits.

"Fine. Here's the truth. Tommy and I did go out a few times," I say slowly, easing into the meat of this tale. "But he never saw the inside of my apartment, let alone my bedroom —or the kitchen island, for that matter."

He narrows his eyes, and a devilish glimmer in them winks at me. "Are you mad about that?"

"No," I answer immediately, leaving no room for misinterpretation or doubt. To further drive my point home, I capture his lips with mine in a dreamy kiss that leaves me sighing in contentment. "We're better off as friends, for sure."

He licks his lips, shifting the pillow beneath his cheek as he watches me.

I blush under his intense stare, especially when flashes of how we almost destroyed my kitchen zip to the forefront of my mind.

Griffin was so passionate and wild.

Right after the Christmas party, I believed our kiss was a magical way to end the year. I figured, even though he didn't turn out to be Prince Charming, our kiss was one for the books.

But the full show was one for the freaking century.

"So, *Little Miss Bumble's Bees*, huh?" He cocks a brow, clearly entertained by just the thought of that story.

"God," I mutter as I bury my face underneath the covers, but he doesn't let me off so easily.

"I want to hear everything," he pushes.

"You really don't," I grumble, but I can't help my laugh. The sound actually comes out more like a snort, though, which makes us both crack up harder.

"Okay!" I relent. "Before I was born, my mom worked as a TV producer. She stepped away when I came along, but she stayed connected. On my eighth birthday, she gave me a *present* of my own show." I roll my eyes, my sarcasm too heavy to hide.

"Why do you say it like that? I think that's any eight-year-old's dream."

"Not mine. All I wanted were Disney rain boots, but no such luck. Instead, I was whisked away to my new set, where I dressed up as a bee, and they called me Katie Bee Bumble. According to my mom, I already had a strong brand with my last name, and the writers couldn't pass up the opportunity to lean into it. So, every week, I studied scripts instead of science textbooks, and the kids at school teased me for the antennas I wore in the show, where I'd go on adventures during pollinating season."

"That's very... educational. You should be... proud." Griffin's face turns red, assumingly from holding in more laughter—at my expense.

But I can't blame the guy. This is almost as ridiculous as my cow painting.

"What exactly happened to little Katie Bee?" He grins.

"She was canceled after two years, and my mother was definitely more outraged than I was. I did get used to the life, though, and I even enjoyed it after the first few months. But looking back now, I know it was for the best. I was a ten-year-old who thought the only way bottled water arrived was sparkling and from an assistant." I shake my head, super embarrassed of my young mind.

"I think we need to watch Katie Bee in action. Please tell me you have the episodes somewhere in this apartment?"

"Not a chance. But can I interest you in a delightful Christmas movie called *All Snowed Inn*, starring the one-and-only Hollie Berry and Ian Brock?" I sit upright, adjusting my pajama sweater back into place over my shoulder. "Funny story—Ian is my friend's friend's boyfriend. Small world, huh?"

He blinks, temporarily dropping the curiosity in my TV stardom. "I didn't follow that..."

"Doesn't matter." I throw the blanket to the side and slide out of bed to grab the remote from the dresser. It tends to travel with me as I get ready, and I'm surprised I haven't lost it completely. I flip through the apps until I find the Adored Network, then pause.

The stupid network took down Hollie's movies after they fired her for living her life.

Which takes me back to my current situation—the scandal

that kept Griffin from meeting me in the first place. The lawsuit is the reason he kept his distance.

"Hey, so, back to the truth I shared earlier..." I face him and bite my lip. "Do you think I was wrong? Should I have told my student to draw something else for the show? Because I was going to. I just couldn't make the suggestion after she told me the meaning behind it. It was just too special for her."

He leans his back against the headboard and clasps his hands in front of him over the comforter. I imagine it's similar to how he sits in a deposition, but he's far less clothed here.

Griffin almost looks normal—if *normal* means satiny coffee brown hair, a constant twinkle in his eye and edge in his tone, and a skilled mouth that knows its way around my mouth.

"I would've done the same as you," he finally says.

I leap onto the bed with a bounce, feeling a lot better and lighter about what I'm going to ask. "What if you talk to your client?"

He stiffens, and his unwavering gaze instantly causes swirls of nausea in my stomach as his shadow of sympathy fizzles away.

"You could talk to him and see if he could drop the lawsuit," I explain. "He doesn't realize what my student is going through. I mean, he's putting his own kid under a lot of stress with this lawsuit, on top of all the other drama he's causing. If he were suing me for something more valid, I wouldn't ask you—"

"But you are asking me, and I told you I don't want to get involved." His knuckles turn white where they remain interlocked over the comforter.

"That was before, though." A nervous chill trickles down my spine, straightening my posture as I say, "I thought you agreed with me. That I'm not in the wrong."

"I said I would've done the same, not that it wasn't wrong."

"So, you *do* think I'm wrong?"

"I didn't say that, either."

"Then what are you saying?" I drop my feet onto the floor and stand, folding my arms across my chest.

"I don't want to lose an important client, Katie, especially not over something that has nothing to do with me." He finally loosens his hands and runs his palms over the comforter, stretching his back as he leans forward.

If I weren't so furious with him, I'd unabashedly revel in the way his corded muscles flex with the movement, blinking and waving at me.

"I meant what I said before. I haven't been able to stop thinking about you or kissing you since the party, but it doesn't change our situation outside this apartment." He slips out from beneath the covers and rises to his full height.

"So, this was an empty fuck just to get it out of our systems then," I state, done with my questions. "Good to know."

"Don't put words in my mouth," he says, but it's more of a plea. "This wasn't a one and done for me, but I need to be smart about this moving forward."

Scoffing, I'm suddenly acutely aware I'm half-naked and exposed, so I spin on my heel in search of pants and a bra.

My heart thunders in my ears.

Hot rage courses through my veins.

And the sting of betrayal slices through my whole body.

I whip out a pair of red and green pajama pants from my dresser drawer. They're my festive pair, which will be completely wasted on this disastrous evening, but I'm too blinded by my anger to look for another.

I'm also too furious to remember how to dress myself with ease, given my struggle to get my foot through the first pant leg. After two failed attempts, I'm adding *embarrassment* to the list of grievances for tonight.

In fact, I have an entire list for this Christmas similar to

Santa's Nice and Naughty List, except mine is full of ugly nuisances.

"Do you need help with those?" Griffin shifts his weight to his left side, and it takes more strength than every reindeer pulling Santa's sleigh to keep myself from getting my fill of his naked torso.

I deeply inhale and shake my head.

With one more forced tug, I get my foot through the opening—*huzzah!*

Now for the second.

"We just met, Katie. Is it really so terrible of me to consider what it could cost my career?"

"Please, stop." From where I'm bent at the waist, the plaid material bunched in one hand, I hold my other up. "You're making this worse."

"I'm trying to explain."

"You're doing a shitty job of it." I give up on the pants and stand upright, tears building in my eyes. "I'm a good person, and I'm a damn great teacher. All I did was encourage my students to express themselves honestly and openly. You're not doing either, by the way, so I guess that means we're finished with that whole ruse."

He flinches, but he doesn't otherwise respond.

"I stand by my actions," I continue. "I've never been anything but truthful when it comes to what I believe is right and fair."

"You're being unfair right now," he whispers.

"And you're being an asshole. That's what this comes down to, doesn't it? Old habits and all."

His jaw hardens as he races past me. In the living room, he snatches his clothes, plucking each article one by one from the floor with a vengeance. His shirt ended up on the lamp by the door. When he leans over to yank it back, the lamp falls, busting the bulb right out of it.

"Fuck," he mutters.

I stumble over my pants as I meet him in the living room, where I finish putting them in place. "Thanks for that."

"I'm leaving." He jerks his clothes into place faster than I've ever seen a human move, albeit they're haphazardly covering him. "Bill me for the damn lamp."

"I won't be speaking to you again, nor will I bill you for my shit," I snap. "I'll take care of it, just as I'll take care of myself."

With one arm through his coat, he whirls around, his face and neck flushed with obvious frustration. "You're accusing me of an awful lot right now, but you're the one who couldn't wait to ask me for a favor. I should be accusing you of sleeping with me just so I could help you out of your predicament."

"Excuse me?" I screech at a pitch not even bats could comprehend.

"Maybe you're not so innocent, after all," he clips and licks angry drops of saliva from his lips.

That same mouth was worshipping me just moments ago, but he's now accusing me of using him. Of being so desperate and deceitful to resort to such disgusting tactics.

"You still don't trust me," I whisper, realizing there's a lot more at play here than his career. At his core, Griffin simply doesn't believe me enough to stick up for me.

Given how strongly he defended me with my sleazy lawyer earlier, I thought I would get that same impulse to protect me once he found out the truth about my art show, but it was futile for me to think the best of him.

"I don't need you to believe me." I jab my finger in his chest to the rhythm of my anthem. "I'm claiming my fucking coal and believing in myself."

"I don't know what that means."

"I don't have to explain myself to you or anyone."

"Horace won't stop. I'm his family lawyer and not affiliated with this lawsuit, but I can assure you, he's not going to let this go."

"Good thing I'm not your problem, then. Just go." I nod toward the door, bracing myself for the moment he slams it behind him.

It's going to hurt like hell, but I don't want him in my apartment anymore.

Buttoning his coat, he looks more like he did earlier this evening when I ran into him at Tracy's—a pretentious businessman with the kind of cold heart molded by selfish drive and determination.

The fact that I don't recognize him as the chivalrous man I spent the last couple hours with makes it easy to let him storm out of my apartment.

But it doesn't ease the nausea burning through my stomach.

Griffin cared so much about my lawyer disrespecting me on the phone earlier. Enough to defend me and go so far as to threaten him. How could he not care that the whole world is doing the same?

The worst part is that I've known what kind of man he is. I've known from the start, and I was stupid enough to think he could be better. That he could be caring and supportive.

It's time I see him for who he really is.

CHAPTER
Eight

GRIFFIN

DAINTY HANDS CLAWING at my shoulders with hunger.

Hot mouth panting my name in my ear.

The heated touch of an insatiable woman.

The fucking memories gnaw at me more and more with every hour that passes.

Katie and I connected on a level I didn't know existed. I was someone else entirely with her—impulsive, vulnerable, and open.

I didn't hold back, nor did I cling to the mask I wear just to get through a day at work.

She made it through to my heart, but everything crashed all around us in a dumpster fire of insecurities and desperation.

"I'm such a dick. A logical one, but a dick, nonetheless," I practically growl as I set the weights on the floor by my feet and sit upright. Between my heavy pants and racing heart, my voice sounds unlike me.

Or, the savagely hoarse tone is exactly me.

After what happened with Katie, I'm not sure who or what I am anymore.

It all happened in such a fucking blur. One that still haunts me now, a couple days later.

I haven't heard from her, and I haven't reached out myself. What would I say, anyway? Sure, I could apologize for being a dick, but I don't think she'd give me the same courtesy. She definitely wouldn't agree that I had a damn point.

"Why?" Miles rises from the bench next to me. "Because you didn't call me the morning after our date? Or because you slept with Katie, the woman your client is suing, then accused her of using you to clear her name before you stormed off?"

An angry gust of an exhale surges through my flared nostrils as I glare at my so-called friend. "I regret going out for beers, or whatever you consider to be our *date*."

"No, you don't. I'm your only friend in the city."

"I have friends," I insist, but it's weak. "I have plenty of them, and they don't badger me with how much they *fucking love hot wings*."

"I do fucking love hot wings, and I stand by that."

"You don't have to describe eating them while you're destroying a basket." I shake my head, recalling how he talked about wings with red hot sauce slithering down his chin. "You moaned like you were having sex in the middle of the bar."

"I stand by that too." He smacks my aching shoulder and points to the weights. "Your rest is over. Give me fifteen more."

I follow his order and heave the dumbbells back up for my second set of chest presses, my mind briefly ceasing all self-deprecating thoughts. The nuisances have been on repeat like the broken talking dolls Tracy used to play with. Instead of changing their batteries or turning them off completely, she'd let them repeat the same stuttering tagline just to grate on my nerves.

My nagging thoughts are a million times worse.

I finish my set with a grunt and despise how calm Miles is in every sense. His steady breathing is very different from my erratic one. The asshole isn't working out with me today. Instead, he's here for moral support—or so I thought.

He doesn't seem to be on my side.

"Things with Katie didn't exactly happen the way you described, by the way," I say, my words clipped from each labored pant. "You would've accused her of the same if you were in my position."

"Maybe." He shrugs. "Or maybe I would've been more understanding and given her the benefit of the doubt. Not all people are evil, man."

"I never said they were, but if you had my job, you wouldn't be so quick to defend everyone."

He chuckles, and it pisses me off.

"What?" I snap as beads of sweat skid down my cheeks like snow in an avalanche.

"I know it's easy for me to talk a big game. After all, I'm on the outside, and I don't completely understand your situation with Katie. It just seems like you have deep, true feelings for her."

I remain quiet.

"Thought so." He nods knowingly. "Would it really be so terrible to ask your client to back off? What's the worst that could happen?"

"This isn't *my* case. It's not my job to ask him," I argue. "Besides, he's the one well-connected client I've been entrusted with, and if I piss him off, he'll take my chances of making partner someday with him when he finds new representation. My job right now is to be a team player, and I can't do that if I let my personal life get the best of me."

"You hate your job," he states so plainly I almost miss the weight of his comment, which is more like a revelation.

"I don't hate my job," I say, but it comes out as more of a question. As if I'm asking him if I do, in fact, dislike doing what I do.

"Fifteen more." He points to the weights by my feet, and again, I force an exhale as I retrieve them for my last set of chest presses.

Once I'm finished, I walk the dumbbells back to the rack, my thoughts flooding back into my mind like the blood rushing to my chest to aid in muscle repair.

"You were saying?" I stop in front of Miles and place both hands on my hips.

"You always complain about the partners, Warren especially. You've been with them for a few years, and you're still doing their grunt work."

The corners of my brows meet in the middle in confusion.

"Answer me this: where do you see yourself in ten years? Are you still working at the same firm? If so, do you think you'll be happy?"

"Those are a lot of damn questions." I shoot him a pointed stare.

"They're important questions you should consider before you run off the one woman who could be *the* one."

"Why do I have to choose between her and my career at all? Why can't she understand it's unfair to ask me to put myself on the line?"

"That's not what I mean, but either way, from what you've said, it doesn't sound like she's asking you to."

"Then what is she asking?" I shove a hand through my damp hair, frustration racing through my veins faster than the adrenaline from a challenging workout.

Sighing, he tilts his head forward. "You should talk to her and find out."

"What kind of cryptic shit is this?"

"You need a shower before you go anywhere." He exaggerates a grimace, and his purposeful deflection sends a rage through my chest.

"What am I missing, asshole?"

"I need to get to my next session, and you have an art teacher to talk to."

I grind my teeth and march toward the lockers, muttering, "I should really start working out alone" as I pass him.

He shoves me through the door, chuckling with amusement.

I'm so fucking glad he finds my misery and confusion so hilarious—the dick.

In the locker room, I go straight to the sink and wash my hands, then study myself in the mirror as Tracy's words of how much I've changed slam into me.

I am different, and not just on the outside. Sure, I'm more jacked than I was before I moved to New York. I actually care about my diet now too. In high school, I didn't care about fitness or sports. I never played any back then, nor did I follow any professional sports, in general. I was what some might consider a nerd, but I didn't care. I had my circle of friends, my textbooks, and a girlfriend who loved me for the person I was.

I thought she did, anyway.

Something inside me snapped when Megan broke up with me in college.

I thought we were serious—we went to the same college in order to stay together, for fuck's sake—but she ended things a week before Christmas break. That's when she told me about her lab partner.

Maybe it's why I despise this season. That and everyone's cinnamon obsession don't make for the best mix of holiday delight for me. Who could blame me for either?

As I grab a towel and make my way toward the shower, a strong eucalyptus scent washes over me when the door of the sauna opens. I nod to the older gentleman who steps out, recognizing him as a local politician.

He barely glances in my direction, which wouldn't be the first time someone of his caliber has instantly dismissed me.

It's all part of the game and the mind fucks of this city's hierarchy.

I don't take it personally, per usual. Just the opposite. It's natural and even makes me feel like I'm a stitch in the fabric of this city. We all have a role to play, and the disposable character is mine.

This place is a stepping stone to being noticed and becoming something more.

Besides, I have my own merits. I even work out with Miles, who's friends with Carter Fields, Manhattan's favorite billionaire. We even all went out for a beer once.

Would Kansas Griffin be living the dream had he wallowed in self-pity over Megan? Had he stayed in the Midwest? Hell no.

I've changed for the better. My younger self would pat me on the back and fist-bump me for our success. He'd be fucking proud of how well we're thriving here.

But as I step into the steaming hot shower, the water melting away the sweat and tension in my shoulders, a knot grows in my gut.

It churns with disconcerting guilt.

I scrub my face and body, phantom caresses infiltrating my senses. I can practically feel Katie.

And as difficult as it is for me to admit it—I fucking miss her.

She makes me crazy and dizzy, but even arguing with her feels good. I feel like myself.

I'm alive when I'm with her, but it's all ruined.

Unless this lawsuit is sorted, I don't see a way out of it, either.

"You slept with her, then ran off?" Tracy shrieks through the speaker on my phone as my espresso wheezes the last drop into my mug.

"For Christ's sake—she tattled on me?" I throw my head back, exasperation making my head ache—and not from the fluorescent lighting of our office suite's kitchen.

I'm alone, so I speak candidly with my sister, although I already hate where this conversation is headed.

I miss the days when she'd call to gush over how much she enjoyed my company when we visited the Statue of Liberty, or when we tried smoothies from a new shop on the corner close to my apartment.

What happened to those conversations? They were much more pleasant and made me loathe myself a lot less.

"I'm in my thirties," I say on a sigh.

"Okay?"

"I'm not supposed to be dealing with drama like I'm in my teens. I know Katie spends ninety percent of her time with high school kids, but *we* are not in high school, Trace."

Her frustrated sigh is loud and sounds more like static from an old television. "She only called to tell me she won't be coming to my New Year's Eve party, but she wouldn't explain why until I pestered it out of her."

"I'm sure it didn't take much pestering." I set my espresso on the counter, holding the phone to my ear as I lean forward. "After all, she just loves making me out to be a monster."

"I can't say I blame her. You've been nothing but rude, judgmental, and selfish since the blind date incident."

I flinch at the three adjectives my own sister chose to describe me. "I'm assuming she told you why I stood her up in the first place. Yet, you still think I'm the bad guy too?"

"Griff," she starts softly. "I love you, and I know the brother I once knew is still in there, albeit buried beneath kale salads and juices. Seriously, you and I haven't even shared a New York slice of pizza yet because it's *just too greasy*. No human on earth declines pizza as often as you do."

"Are you mad at me for hurting your friend or for the fact that I don't eat pizza? Because you're taking me on a roller coaster of reasons to hate me, and I don't understand any of them."

"I just... Katie really likes you."

I whirl around and rest my hip on the edge of the counter, my stomach lurching.

Does she still really like me?

The question is on the tip of my tongue, but I can't seem to bring myself to ask. I'm paralyzed with the fear that she'll say Katie feels nothing for me now.

And just the thought of that causes a knee-jerk reaction of bile in my throat.

"I thought you really liked her too. It's why I paired you two together in the first place." The more she talks, the more discouraged her tone grows, and it absolutely guts me. "I just wish you could work your shit out."

A commotion filtering from the main offices pulls my attention in that direction.

"I need to get back to work." I grab the mug and sip the bitter liquid.

"Are you coming to my place on Christmas Eve for dinner with Mom and Dad?" she asks, hope lifting her pitch by the end of her question. "They keep asking me, and I keep stalling. They don't think they're going to see you at all during their visit."

"I'll be there," I relent, although I'm not sure how I'll make it happen. Not with the workload waiting for me. It somehow continues growing with every passing day.

But I don't mention any of this to my sister. Instead, we end the call on that positive note, and I make my way down the short and narrow hall toward my office.

I'm two feet from it when I hear more noise. Laughter and music erupt from Warren's office as I set my mug on my desk. I'll come back for it.

Curiosity drags me toward Warren's. He said he'd be visiting family in Connecticut until after Christmas, so he piled paperwork onto my desk.

The ass didn't even have the courtesy to ask or notify me via email. Instead, he left a Post-it, which simply read "Finish ASAP."

"Hey! It's Cinnamon Toast *Fail*," Warren slurs as I come to a halt in the doorway of his office.

A few people I've never seen before mill about the space, which is three times the size of mine. They each have a short glass in one hand and a cigar in the other, little puffs of smoke surrounding them.

"You're not supposed to smoke in here," I say.

"What does the door say?" Warren points his cigar toward it, and it's not until I turn to look that I realize he's being a smartass. What else did I expect? "It's my name on there. I can do what I want, okay, rookie?"

With a tight-lipped smile, I retreat, but I don't get too far before he speaks up again.

"What are you even doing here this late, Chase?" Warren calls out.

"You told me you'd be in Connecticut, so I've been working on the cases you gave me."

A couple of the other guys raise their eyebrows and snicker into their drinks.

What the hell is so funny?

"Yeah—I definitely lied about that." Warren pops the cigar into his mouth, lights the end of it, then follows it up with several succinct puffs. "Thanks to you, I can partake in the fun things about this job. Keep it up, slugger."

My boss winks at me and returns to laughing with his friends.

They're laughing *at* me.

My blood boils.

Every vessel in my body threatens to burst as my vision blurs through twitching eyes.

Miles was right. I hate this stupid, degrading job. Most of all, I despise working for the condescending prick in front of me—the same asshole I, myself, have turned into.

It ends now.

"I quit," I blurt, but it's not loud enough to grab their attention.

As I ball my fists at my sides, Warren finally looks over his shoulder, cigar still sticking out of his mouth. "Are you still here?"

"I fucking quit, Warren," I assert, my enunciation crisper than keys on a typewriter.

No words have ever felt more satisfying than the ones I just slung at the bastard.

Spinning on my heel, I race to my office for my personal effects, my blood pumping with the thrilling anticipation of exiting this building as a free man.

On my way, I nearly trip over a string of garland that fell from its place and onto the floor, but I don't let the small misstep stop me.

Nothing can, now that I've set this in motion.

"What did you just say?" Warren hisses from the open door.

"You heard me, but here. Let me write it down for you." I grab a pad of Post-its from my drawer, scribble out, *I fucking quit*, and hold it up for him. "Are we all clear now?"

Both eyes bug out of his head as they bounce from the note to me and back. "You can't... go. You can't... quit," he sputters, his blotchy neck lighting on fire with an oncoming tantrum. "Don't be an idiot!"

If I wasn't so damn pleased before, I certainly am now.

I've never heard my hoity-toity boss have so much difficulty spitting out a sentence.

"What would've made me an idiot is choosing you and this firm over the woman I love. Now *that* would be stupid." Smug victory filling my body, I clap a hand to his burning cheek and give it a smack. "Enjoy doing your own work, *slugger*. I'm out."

"Love? You're leaving for love? You never get out of this office. How did you fucking manage to fall in love?" he calls out.

I leave him with a parting wink just before the elevator doors shut, and I travel down to the first floor, where I glide through the lobby with a grin on my face.

Sure, this might be completely rash and crazy and so very unlike me, but it doesn't mean I'm wrong to quit and fight for Katie. The latter definitely doesn't feel wrong.

Our connection is life-upending, and the rush of emotions rolling through my body right now is beyond anything I imagined this would feel like.

She and I might've only known each other for a week, but these past seven days have had more of an impact on me than anything else I've experienced.

I mean, I was with my previous ex for over a year and couldn't figure out how I felt about her until she was ready for the next step. I was never sure about anyone before Katie.

With her, a week is all I've needed to be certain.

Outside, Christmas lights wrap around every tree in sight and shine a touch brighter, especially against the night sky.

It's probably just me, but even the people power walking to their final destination seem to slow down, a new bounce in each step.

I inhale what feels like the first breath of fresh air I've taken since stepping foot into this state.

And when I climb into an available taxi, I know exactly where I need to go.

CHAPTER
Nine

KATIE

"I'M CLAIMING MY COAL," I say to my reflection in the mirror. "*Eh.*"

I snatch a ponytail holder from my drawer and smooth my hair back to better see my face. Once my long, tangled strands are secure, I lick my lips and try again. "I'm claiming my coal."

I squint, still dissatisfied with my personal pep talk. I just don't *feel* it.

All I'm feeling is crappy sadness over the blowup with Griffin.

Erin's sent me inspirational quotes for days, and each one is more ridiculous than the last. They actually make me laugh, which I think is the reason for her relentless string of texts, so I have to appreciate them. It's the main way she knows how to be supportive.

Tracy has also offered her shoulder to lean on, but Griffin's her brother. It's hard to call him a hardheaded dingbat to her face.

Then again, he's not the only one at fault for the mess

we've made. I'm to blame too, aren't I? I asked him for a favor the second we fell into bed together. I gave him a damn good reason to doubt me, and I shouldn't have been so taken aback when he jumped on it. After all, he thought I'd purposely tried to kill him at the Christmas party.

I thought we'd moved past that, though.

We had sex in my kitchen, for crying out loud!

But clearly, our night together never mattered to him. I was just another lay to the haughty jackass, and I need to accept that.

Shaking my body loose, I jostle the doubt to the back of my mind. This is not the time to question my value or integrity. I have to find another lawyer before my hearing next week, and I need to be prepared.

Confidence and self-assurance are key.

Which means I can't continue sobbing over my best friend's callous brother.

I blow out an exhale, then work through a few mouth and voice exercises I learned as a child star. I was an actress. It was eons ago, but it should be like riding a bike, right?

So, I can *act* confident and self-assured, even if I don't feel it.

"Fuck it," I mutter.

Once I grab the comfortable robe off the hook on the back of my bathroom door, I also snatch a pair of knee-high fuzzy socks. I go to the kitchen for wine, and then I settle into my bed with the TV volume on low.

This is totally the night of champions.

After a few minutes, I check the time on my phone and decide to get this over with. Scrolling through my calls, I click on the one I'm looking for and brace myself.

"Hi, darling," my mom answers.

It's Friday, which means I'm upholding our weekly tradition of chatting on the phone. Unlike the other times, though,

I'm now sitting on my bed in a fluffy robe, which is redder than anything in Mrs. Claus's closet.

I bet jolly St. Nick's wife is not drinking cheap wine straight from the bottle, though.

"Hey, Mom," I say on a sigh and wipe the stream of runaway wine from the corner of my mouth. But a couple stubborn drops land on the flap of my robe. At least it's the same color as the cabernet, so maybe they're not so obvious. Who's going to see me like this, anyway?

"I so badly wanted to surprise you this weekend with a little quality mother-daughter time at the spa, but I sadly couldn't make it."

I draw my brows together. It's hard to believe she had any such plans, especially with her big powdered milk audition coming up early next week.

"You'll never believe what happened to me," she continues. "My dog walker up and quit on me a few days ago, so I've had to walk Cinny all on my own this week. I've been swamped."

I sit up, but it's not because I feel her pain. It's because of her dog.

Cinny is short for Cinnamon, and instantly, I think of Griffin.

Of his smoldering glare.

His laugh.

The way he held me in this very bed.

Why did I have to invite him up here that night? I could've just sent him on his way before things got so infuriatingly complicated.

Before sex with him cemented his touch on my skin and his memory in my heart.

"Are you there, darling?" my mom asks, and I'm shocked she stopped talking long enough to realize how silent I am.

"I'm here. What were—"

A knock on my front door interrupts us, and I check the

time again to see it's almost midnight. Who could be visiting at this hour?

"As I was saying," my mom carries on as I tiptoe toward the door. "I had to use a thin plastic bag to pick up Cinny's stool like a common..."

My mom rambles on as if I'm in any way part of the conversation. It's how she is, though, and as much as I'd like her to fully support me for once—she hasn't even asked about my blind date or what's happened since—it's no use.

She is the way she is, resentment of love and all. Part of her attitude against the sentiment has sprinkled into my own perception too, but I never stopped believing I could—and would—find someone.

It's why I so foolishly kissed a stranger under a damning piece of mistletoe last weekend.

Another knock sounds, cutting through my thoughts and my mom's story about a food truck vendor, who she claims was too shy to ask for her autograph, but she knew he recognized her. I would've hung up on her already, but in the case of there being a serial killer at my apartment, I need to have it on record.

Living alone in New York City makes me think about stuff like that.

But I stop listening entirely as I check the peephole and see who's on the other side.

A tiny gasp escapes my parted lips as I clutch the phone to my ear with a firm grip. "Mom, I need to go," I say, and I don't wait for her reply.

I end the call and curl my fingers around the doorknob.

Steeling myself, I swing the door open and come face to face with pleading brown eyes, swirls of whiskey drawing mesmerizing patterns in the dark irises. Lashes matching in color fan around them with ease, and my breath catches.

Griffin.

"What're you doing here?" I ask, cautiously blocking him from entering.

He shoves his free hand through his thick hair, and one section of it sticks up with stubborn resilience, much like Griffin himself. "I don't want to be an asshole," he says as he waves the red rose in his hand. "I don't want to be like the Warrens of the world. I don't want to keep putting my career and reputation before the people who matter to me."

The blood in my veins hums, pulsing through my body until my heart beats to a new rhythm. The more he talks, the harder I fall.

And the more I want to leap into his arms.

"You matter to me, Katie. You might drive me insane, but God, do I fucking love it." He steps toward me, licking his lips. "I love *you*."

I cover my mouth with trembling hands. Is this real? "What about the lawsuit? Your client and—"

He shakes his head. "Right after I quit my job, I talked to Horace."

"You did what?" I drop my hands back to my sides, and my jaw drops along with them. His entire proclamation doesn't make sense to me.

This can't be real...

"Horace won't be pursuing the lawsuit. He's dropping the whole thing." His grin is expectant as he searches my eyes with hope in his own, but I'm having a hard time processing all this.

I'd say it's a Christmas miracle, but the way things have been going so sideways for me lately, it's hard to believe in such magic.

But Griffin is here, nonetheless, telling me everything I've wanted to hear since before I met him.

"But how? How did you convince him to do this?" I blink back tears.

"I spoke to him honestly and openly. I spoke from the

heart, and he did the same until we got down to the root of it all."

"I don't understand."

"I'd love to explain, but could we talk inside?" He chuckles.

It makes a watery burst of soft laughter rip from my clogged throat. Once I invite him in and close the door, I lean my back against it, still unsure about what to make of all this.

I also wish I wasn't wearing this robe, with wine stains on the flap. I'm sure my hair is flying in all directions, halfway up and down, which isn't on purpose.

There's nothing I can do about those, but I at least swipe at the corners of my mouth for any chocolate residue from the sweets stash I dipped into.

"Horace is going through a divorce, and he was simply trying to prove he could be there for his son. To show up for him. He jumped on the first opportunity to do so, although he was severely misguided." His previously smiling lips morph into a firm frown. "We can blame the overwhelming stress of breaking up a family for that."

"I can definitely understand his situation. My parents divorced when I was young, and they both did questionable things to win me over. My dad adopted an elephant in my name, and my mom got me my own show." I lift one shoulder and quickly drop it.

"I've learned enough from this profession to use it to my advantage. I convinced him to see what he was doing was wrong and could potentially push his son further away." He steps toward me, the rose still in his hold at his side. "I also had help from you. Being with you has opened my eyes to who I was becoming, and I don't want to be that guy. He fucking sucks."

I laugh as a single tear rolls down my cheek.

"Seriously, the guy is obsessed with salads and juices. It's not healthy." His grin spreads, as does my own.

"Thank you for what you did for me," I say sincerely. "You didn't have to, and I shouldn't have asked. I should've respected your boundaries, and—"

"They were stupid boundaries." One side of his lip lifts into a shy half-grin.

"You literally fixed all my problems. I mean, the board is still mad at me, but it's nothing a little Christmas cheer won't take care of, right?"

"I agree." He winks, and my stomach does backflips. "And I'm sorry."

"I'm sorry too," I whisper, and the tension from the last couple nights seeps out of my tightly wound muscles.

"I believe I owe you a rose." He offers me the flower, and I gladly take it, my smile making my cheeks sore. "One more thing…"

"Yes?"

"I'd really like to kiss you now."

I finally leap into his arms, which is what I've wanted to do since I saw him standing on the other side of my door.

He meets me in the middle for a searing kiss while I wrap my legs around him, my body buzzing with need.

I drop the rose onto the counter as Griffin walks us backward, his lips stuck on mine like magnets. It's pure bliss.

What's better is when he lays me back on my bed, pushes my legs open, and climbs onto his knees, his unwavering gaze boring into mine with lust and determination.

"I'm going to make all this up to you," he promises. "I'm fucking in love with you."

I squirm underneath him, my breasts pressed against his hard chest as I attempt to control the heat in my core. Hearing him say he loves me makes the butterflies in my stomach dance with glee.

My heart swells.

"Before you showed up tonight, I was one glass of wine

away from searching the neighborhood for stray cats to love on."

He captures my smiling lips with his own, paying extra attention to my bottom lip and nibbling on it.

"Thank you for coming to my rescue in more ways than one," I murmur as the air shifts. As the room spins with dizzying lust and the anticipation of spending tonight with Griffin.

Of waking up on Christmas morning in his arms.

The thought of every day being like that floods my chest with warm and fuzzy feelings.

"I love you," I say and cup both his cheeks in my small hands as I kiss him.

I writhe beneath him, struggling for release, even though we're still dressed. We have all night, after all, but the sudden urgency to have him right now consumes me.

He seems to feel it too. The wild way he paws at my clothes is ravenous and downright sexy, especially since he peppers kisses along every sliver of skin he exposes.

I do the same to him until we're completely bare, rolling around the bed, my mattress squeaking like it's clapping for our reunion.

I am too.

Straddling his hips, I climb on top and grip his hard length, filthy plans of what I'd like to do to him filling my mind.

"Fuck, Katie," Griffin hisses, twitching in my hold.

With an impish grin, I roll a condom on, then rise onto my knees and guide him to my dripping, desperate entrance.

We gasp in sync as I sink onto him, and he fills me to the hilt.

"Yes," I breathe, my eyelids fluttering from the friction of his rigid shaft along my tight walls.

"Ride me faster. Harder. Just... fuck me," he strains and slides his palms up my thighs.

Griffin Chase is at my mercy, and it's more delicious than any decadent holiday dessert.

I've been claiming my coal this season and happy to be on the naughty list, but nothing about him or us feels as such.

Well, the naughty part works in my favor, at least.

But this is more like a reward, and I bask in it as I do what he says.

The heated desire weighing on his hooded gaze fuels me to move more sensually.

More purposefully.

I move my hips at a tantalizingly slow pace, reveling in the feel of him as I slide forward and backward, up and down, gyrating above him.

We move together, connected as we make love.

At the beginning of this holiday season, I didn't think love would find me, but all it took was a kiss under the mistletoe with a stranger. He turned out to be my enemy, but in the end, Griffin is simply *the one*.

Epilogue

GRIFFIN

"IT WOULD LOOK BETTER HERE, THOUGH," I say, holding up the canvas painting she did of a holiday gingerbread couple.

Katie says it's us, which is why the gingerbread man wears a tie and a scowling grimace similar to the likes of the Grinch. The girl is the complete opposite and smiles brightly, a string of lights hanging around her neck.

"You could actually see it here," I insist. "Otherwise, we need to take the cow painting in your room down and put this up in there. It's much better."

She fakes a gasp of offense. "Don't be mean to Moo-lan."

"You named it?" I jerk my head around, a laugh caught in my throat.

"Is that a dealbreaker?" She points between us, highly amused with a curvy arch in her brow.

"Not in the slightest." I wrap my free arm around her midsection and brush my lips across the column of her neck. "It makes me love you even more."

It's true. Katie is quirky, and I can't get enough. It's what makes her so exciting, and by association, she makes me more fun too.

I like the guy I'm becoming since I met her a couple weeks ago.

I may be unemployed and wearing snowflake socks that match my girlfriend's, but I'm shockingly fine with it all.

This feels like the right path.

I have a host of new possibilities in front of me. In fact, Horace himself is so appreciative of my assistance to help him see the light, so to speak, he's offered to connect me to his legal contacts for any open positions after the holidays.

Katie's had some good professional fortune too. With the lawsuit dropped and the local media focusing on the "Santa Bandit," instead, Katie's slowly retreating from the public eye. It's been hard to find new stories on her at all these days, and the two new ones we've stumbled across actually praise her for refusing to stifle her students' perspectives.

It's about time someone reported on her merits.

The board of her school has taken notice of it all as well. They've dropped any discussions of letting her go. The principal called yesterday to give her the news and congratulate her, his British accent heavy with excitement.

It's honestly astounding how fast things can change in a matter of a few days. Surprisingly enough, I'm even starting to believe there is something quite special about Christmas.

"It's too cluttered there," Katie argues and wiggles her nose as she tries to find another good spot for the new painting. "There are too many gingerbread men in the kitchen. We need to spread them out."

Now it's my turn to exaggerate a gasp. "Is there really such a thing as too many?"

Several of the little cookie men, assumingly accumulated over several years, are scattered around the open room. There's even a gingerbread cat on the wall next to the refrigerator, and underneath it reads the line "Oh, Meow!" instead of "Oh, Snap!"

But there are a lot of other Christmas items too. In the nearby corner is a white tin holding a few spatulas, one of which reads "Let there be peas on Earth." It has two peas on it, and they're wearing Santa hats and holding hands. Next to it is a spatula with a snowman on it that reads "Spread the frosting."

Katie loves corny quotes almost as much as Tracy. It's one of the many things they bond over, and it makes me laugh when they squeal over a new addition.

"You're right." She throws her hands up. "There can never be too many."

I cup my hand around my ear and lean forward. "I'm sorry, what was that? Did you actually admit I'm right for once?"

"Never." Her cheeks turn a light shade of pink as she clearly holds in a laugh.

It's a similar look to the one she wears when she's holding in a sneeze, which is something I've learned about her since I showed up on her doorstep with a single rose in my hand and my heart on the sleeve of my crisp button-up.

I've gotten to know so much about Katie, and each piece of her that I uncover, I fall harder.

I'm a crazy man in love.

I never understood the concept before, but as I'm living it now, I certainly get the magnitude of it.

"Come here." I cup the back of her neck, her blonde tresses tangled in my fingers, and I plant a heated kiss to her lips.

The sweet taste of red velvet pancakes from our breakfast lingers on her tongue, and I lap it up.

Moaning, she pulls back. "I know where this is headed, but we have to head over to Tracy's soon."

"Okay, but what do I do with this dashing couple?" I return my focus to the painting of the gingerbread couple.

I actually care about where it goes, which again, isn't something I would've stewed over a month ago, but here I am.

Because if it matters to Katie, it matters to me.

Anything to make her rosy cheeks bounce when she smiles.

"Are you sure about introducing me to your parents tonight?" She bites her lip, and I use my thumb to pull the flesh out from beneath her teeth.

"Like I said earlier, I wouldn't have asked if I wasn't serious." I place another kiss to her mouth and get back to work.

Once the painting is in place above a wooden "Recipe for Christmas" sign, I stand back to admire our handy work.

"Voila," I announce. "What do you think?"

"I like it, and as much as I love how pleased you are with yourself, it's time we get ready to go to your sister's. We still have to help her set up for the family dinner."

"How did I get roped into all this decorating today?"

"Because I promised you steaming hot sex on the balcony tonight." She winks over her cup of coffee as she tilts it back for a final sip.

"Were you serious about that?" I blink, and the strain in my pants is instant.

"If you promise not to growl and bark like a bear during mating season. I'm seriously surprised my neighbor didn't bang on the wall last night to shush us."

I quirk a brow. "At least I don't sound like a lost bat."

"Is this how it's going to be? We're going to argue over who makes the worst sounds during sex?"

"Not only that, but we're also going to have a ton of sex just to gather more evidence to use in said arguments."

"I do like the sound of that, specifically the *ton of sex* part." She wiggles her eyebrows suggestively.

Her face is free of any makeup, and her eyes glow. It's my favorite look of hers.

It's even better when she settles on top of me, wearing nothing but this expression as she straddles my lap. Which is how she woke me up this morning.

She pinches the fabric of my shirt and draws me closer. "Not sure if I've mentioned this before, but I like when you wear sweatpants. Your suits are hot, but this look is... sexy." She licks her lips and leaves a sheen across them, the pink flesh glistening and enticing me to pull her flush against me.

I hold her close as I lean down to brush my lips against hers, whispering, "I like when you talk French while I fuck you."

She did so this morning, and I lost my damn mind.

Katie wraps her arms around my neck and clasps her fingers there as she hums in pleasure. "I have something."

"Yes, please. Should I meet you in the bedroom, or will you give me my Christmas gift right here on the counter again?" I ask, my sensual implication of getting naked right here loud and clear.

She smacks my chest and chews on her cheek as she searches the box by her bare feet. The festive green polish on her toes makes me grin as she rises again, something hidden in her hand.

"The suspense is killing me..." I reach around her waist to grab whatever's behind her back, but she squeals and twists her body away from me.

"You're the most impatient man!" She giggles as I pin her against the nearest wall.

"I am when it comes to you." I peer into her eyes, and she stops squirming, her lips frozen halfway open and teasing me.

A strand of hair is draped across her nose, and I gently swipe it away, my fingertips caressing her smooth skin.

She hums again, and the heady sound travels down to my

cock, which surges to life with need for her as she reveals what's in her hand.

"Is that what I think it is?" I ask, my question full of awe.

She nods slowly and raises the leafy green bunch, a red ribbon tied around the top, until it hangs over our heads. "It's the mistletoe we shared our first kiss under. I stole it from Tracy's while she complained about burning another batch of sugar cookies the other day."

"You're amazing." I engulf her delicate cheek in my wolfish palm, and we share another kiss under the mistletoe in the middle of her apartment.

Beady gingerbread eyes stare back at us, but I can't stop kissing her.

It's hard to keep my hands off her at all.

And I know I want to share all my kisses with Katie.

The End

Want more of Griffin and Katie? Download the free bonus epilogue here - https://geni.us/SUTMBonus

Curious as to how Erin ended up with the hot British principal? Read her story in Stuck with the Boss (free in KU) here - https://geni.us/SWTBoss

Polish your jingle bells, strategically hang the mistletoe, and get ready to claim your spot on The Naughty List. This holiday season, fourteen of your favorite authors are spicing up the cocoa and taking advantage of those long winter nights, proving that sometimes it's more fun to claim your coal than it is to stay on Santa's good side. After all, well-behaved women might make the nice list, but naughty ones have all the fun…

Grab the Whole Series here: https://geni.us/TNLSeries

Wood Girl Gone Bad by Mae Harden

Owned By Santa by Imani Jay

Stuck Under the Mistletoe by Georgia Coffman

Lovestruck by Julia Jarrett

Secret Santa Surprise by Tamrin Banks

Checking It Twice by Claire Hastings

Falling for the Grinch by Amy Alves

Unexpected Christmas by Eliza Peake

Sleighed by Em Torrey

Nailed by Claire Wilder

Entry Level by Bella Michaels

Rockin' Around the Christmas Tree by Breanna Lynn

Two Pink Lines for Christmas by Ember Davis

Run Run Rudolph by Chelle Sloan

Also by Georgia Coffman

Stuck with You Series
Stuck with the Billionaire
Stuck with the Movie Star
Stuck with the Boss
Stuck with the Single Dad

Stuck with You Series Spinoffs
Stuck with a Date
Stuck with the Rock Star

Stuck with You Series Holiday Spinoffs
Stuck at Christmas
Stuck Under the Mistletoe

The Heat Series
Falling for a Stranger
Falling for a Player
Falling for a Bachelor
Falling for My Roommate

Standalone Novels
Official
Unbreakable

Acknowledgments

Thank you, reader, for picking up this book. This is the thirteenth (OMG!) story I've published, and this gig never ceases to amaze me. Mainly, YOU never cease to amaze me. I'm so thankful you read my words. Whether this is the first or thirteenth book of mine you've checked out, I appreciate you taking a chance on me.

A big thanks to my editor, Amanda, for helping me polish this book. I had my doubts, but as always, you encouraged me and made these characters shine.

To the KKSB and the other authors in The Naughty List series—thank you all for allowing me to be part of the group! You're all so freaking talented, and I'm grateful to have worked on this project with y'all. It's been a fun ride.

To my mom—thank you for your positivity, your big heart, and your support. Your encouragement never wanes, and I have no words to adequately express my gratitude.

Last but not least, my husband. You're the reason I know anything about happily ever afters. You're my rock, and I couldn't do any of this without you. Thank you for your constant love and support through every book. I love you, forever and always.

About the Author

Georgia Coffman is an author of steamy contemporary romances and romantic comedies. She has a Master's in Professional Writing and loves the TV show *Friends*, as well as shopping. She and her husband enjoy working out and playing with their two pups. Georgia loves to connect on social media or through email, so feel free to reach out with any questions, your fave book recommendations, or even a funny joke!

Newsletter - http://www.georgiacoffman.com/newsletter
Facebook - https://geni.us/GeorgiaFB
Instagram - https://geni.us/GeorgiaIG
TikTok - https://geni.us/GeorgiaTT
Pinterest - https://geni.us/GeorgiaPinterest

Goodreads - https://geni.us/GeorgiaGR
BookBub - https://geni.us/GeorgiaBB
Amazon - https://geni.us/GeorgiaAmazon
Verve Romance - https://geni.us/GeorgiaVerve
Website - www.georgiacoffman.com